A TIME TO FANTASIZE

by

May Kapela Davenport

A BOOK OF PLAYS

md BOOKS
Los Altos Hills, California U.S.A.

i

To my sons
Robin Liloa and Byron Kihei Davenport

First Printing

Cover: The Clowns, 1960, 20x50 oil
by May Davenport

Printed in the United States of America
ISBN 0-9603118-7-4

PREFACE

What is a play? A play is to play. That is, it is a human delight to play, and to read May Davenport's plays is to be delighted.

A Time to Fantasize is a collection of plays written to be read aloud and meant to delight the senses. To fantasize is to imagine, an exercise of the mind which holds perennial delight.

To hear a play is almost as delightful as to see one. It can be even better because we can imagine the details when hearing a play. And it is in exercising imagination that we receive delight.

Human imagination is a wonderful facility which enables us to embellish with marvelous decorations what we hear when a play is read.

We can imagine the setting, the costumes and even the facial expressions of the characters when we listen to a play. This act of imagination is a private process, so that each listener can in his own way embellish the play as read.

Each listener can, by imagination, complete each play in an individual way. That is an additional source of delight for those who hear these plays.

To fantasize may be the exclusive province of the human mind and to allow oneself a time to fantasize is to allow the mind to play, a process certain to delight.

Radio was a delightful invention because it allowed the listener to give free reign to his imagination. While listening to radio plays the mind could roam freely, completing each detail at will. Listening to radio gave one a time to fantasize.

The same delight will ensue as a result of hearing these three plays read. Two of them are "closet plays," a literary term meaning plays that are meant to be heard, but not staged. The third play is a radio play, one which is likewise meant to be heard.

May Davenport offers us a gift. *A Time to Fantasize* is a gift which offers us the delight of exercising our imaginations.

Susan Thorley Schwafel

CONTENTS

PROLOGUE

Sometimes when simple everyday cooking, gardening, even household chores become burdensome, and neither playing my piano nor painting at my easel will help soothe my frustrated, somewhat bruised inner spirit, I like to write about humorous characters for my own entertainment.

In my world of fiction my characters recall imaginary, exciting foreign adventures. They visualize people in colorful native costumes. They feel the need of trust and communication, and they solve their problems in their own individual ways.

My "closet" plays, written to be read rather than performed, are of many composite persons at home and abroad. In recapturing the essence of English as spoken with a lilting accent, I deliberately misspelled some words. No character's speech or behavior was intended to humiliate any living person.

Laughing at my fictionalized characters' antics, I am able to face a complex, harsh world of reality. If sharing the laughter in this book helps another to function more creatively with his or her responsibility, then my own time to fantasize has not been in vain.

May Kapela Davenport

OF SAILING SHIPS
AND GHOSTLY BEINGS*

(A Fantasy in One Act)

*Originally published in *Two Plays,* Pacifica Publishing
Company, 1976.

CHARACTERS

Pete Kapiolani—A happy, good-natured docent for a group of tourists in Kona, Hawaii.

Tourists—Mr. and Mrs. Smith from Texas wearing shorts and Aloha shirts; Two youthful singles: Antonio from Brazil, and Fifi from Puerto Rico; Two middle-aged singles from New Jersey who enjoy birdwatching; Six retired couples wearing his and her bright, floral muumuus, shirts, coconut hats, oversized sunglasses and thongs. They ad lib a lot with New England, midwestern, and southern accents but often revert back to accents of their great grandparents who migrated to the United States from Sweden, Ireland, England, Scotland, Germany, Russia, France, Italy; A couple from Japan, the woman in a kimono costume, the man in a tropical suit; A couple from the Philippines in their costumes; A couple from Hong Kong, the wife in a Chinese costume and the man with a matching shirt; A couple from Korea in their costumes.

Joe Kalama—The bus driver who loves to sing and play the ukelele.

Chiefess Kalehua—An impetuous Hawaiian ghost who plays the calabash expertly while speaking to herself, just as naturally as someone today speaks on a phone to someone and drums his fingers unconsciously.

Captain Cook—A tall, middle-aged, irascible ghost. With wig, hat, sword and holster, he reminds one of an irate George Washington crossing the Delaware.

Mrs. Palama—An uninhibited, eccentric Hawaiian hula teacher and expert chanter.

Mrs. Malama—Another hula teacher and expert chanter.

Others—James Cook in his teens, Cook's parents, 2 brothers; James Cook in his late twenties, Admiral, 2 seamen; Ghostly Royal Hawaiian chief and his entourage of high priest, Kahili bearers, 4 ancient Hawaiian drummers, 16 torch bearing modern-dancer-warriors, 8 hula dancers for ancient hulas with sticks, stones, calabash, uliulis, and 7 chiefesses in sparkling, transparent costumes representing 7 islands of Hawaii.

ACT I
Scene I

The Scene:

An imaginary site in Kealakekua Bay in Kona, Hawaii. UPSTAGE-RIGHT is a trail leading to a volcanic cliff dotted with inaccessible caves. To the left of the cliff in the background is a panoramic view of Mauna Kea in the distance, Mauna Loa in the foreground, and a smoking Kilauea crater in between the two mountains. UPSTAGE-CENTER is a rocky hill, contoured in front to seat the ghostly Royal Hawaiian Chief and his entourage. UPSTAGE-LEFT is a coconut grove. DOWNSTAGE-LEFT is a weather-beaten rowboat with oars. DOWNSTAGE-RIGHT is a thatched hut with open sides. Under the eaves hang two calabashes in knotted raffia holders. Vines and flowers cascade from the calabashes. To the right of the hut is a post with the glowering God Ku on the top, and below, arrows with mileages to Mauna Loa, Mauna Kea, Kilauea Crater, Hilo, City of Refuge, and Captain Cook's Monument. It is a balmy day in the summer of 1976.

Stage Directions:

As the curtain opens, offstage music is heard on Pete's portable tape recorder, which he carries. *(Taped music suggested is: "He Inoa No Kaiulani," sung by Nina from the record de Mello arr- Melway, Inc., Music of Polynesia, Inc.)* Enter DOWNSTAGE-RIGHT Pete Kapiolani followed jauntily by a parade of tourists humming and marching to the music, joining in the chorus of "E Ha Ha" with gusto. As Pete leads the group UPSTAGE-CENTER to gape at the caves in the cliff, the following break away to various positions.

(DOWNSTAGE-RIGHT is the retired couple from New England.)

WIFE

Kayaler-kekooer Bay ... what a beauty spot. Imagine, Captain Cook discovering this in 1776, no 1777, no ... 1778 about the same time my great, great, great...

HUSBAND

(Interrupting.) god fearing ancestors were sailing to Boston. *(He laughs as his wife clobbers him playfully.)* My ancestors came over on the Mayflower, too, 'cause they didn't want to go to jail in England.

WIFE

(Peeved.) Come along jailbird...

(DOWNSTAGE-RIGHT overhearing the New England couple is the retired couple from the south.)

WIFE

Dem Mayflowah peeple sure talk funny. *(Mimics.)* Kayaler-kekooer Bay ... ha! Everybuddy knows it's *(Overexaggerates.)* Kay-allah-kaykoo-ah.

HUSBAND

Sh-h-h, dey talk jest as funny as we do, but who cares. Dis is Hawaii. Everybody understands each other. *(Busses his wife.)*

(DOWNSTAGE-LEFT Antonio and Fife are holding hands.)

ANTONIO

This place is just like Forteleza in Brazil. Warm ... sunshiny ... sea coast full of jagandas ... that's our sailing raft our fishermen use. Just think. If my ancestors *(Laughs.)* now I'm talking like those Plymouth Rock folks. But, if my ancestors didn't jump ship in Rio de Janeiro ... my navigating ancestors might have jumped ship here in Hawaii.

FIFE

My Spanish ancestors landed in Puerto Rico. And some of the Africans jumped ship there. We get along fine. This place is like Puerto Rico ... trade winds, coconut palms, blue-green ocean and coral beaches. Only ... they make a fuss over shells with holes ... puka shells.

(DOWNSTAGE-CENTER are two bird watchers looking at the seagulls over the audience heads.)

JACK

Seagulls! Millions of seagulls!

HILDA

Fascinating birds ... look at them glide. Must be a school of fish out there.

(DOWNSTAGE-RIGHT Mr. Smith argues with his wife.)

MR. SMITH

Mary, the next time we take another packaged tour, with free hula lessons ... I'm going to have my head examined.

MRS. SMITH

Oh, hon. Isn't this fun?

MR. SMITH

(Mimics.) Isn't this fun? Helluva vacation with a bunch of strange people. We must be crazy, coming on our honeymoon to ... *(Throws his hands up in disgust.)* this tourist town.

MRS. SMITH

Come off it, sweet. With today's prices, nobody would be here 'cept on these packaged tours. I love the hula lessons. *(She sways her hips awkwardly and giggles.)*

MR. SMITH

For the luvva Mike ... *(Looks around uncomfortably.)*

(Pete's tape recording of "He Inoa No Kaiulani" ends. Joe Kalama picks a tune quietly on his ukelele as Pete waves for attention.)

PETE KAPIOLANI

Welcome Malihinis. Hele mai! *(Joe Kalama gives a fast strum for attention on his ukelele and everybody seats himself comfortably UPSTAGE-CENTER.)* Folks, this spot is believed by some old-timers to be haunted. People get lost easily. So far, our hula instructors ... Mrs. Palama and Mrs. Malama ... have taken a short cut from up there ... *(Points to the top of the cliffs.)* to down here. *(There is general laughter.)* Mrs. Palama lived in Kona as a girl, and I'm sure she'll find us. The package tour includes free hula lessons ...

MR. SMITH

Pete ... I can skip the hula lessons. I want to take pictures of real hula dancers to show people back in Texas the beauty of the hands telling the story ... *(General objection by the group who protest in foreign languages that hula-hula lessons are great.)*

PETE KAPIOLANI

Cool it folks! Cool it! *(Joe Kalama gives another fast strum for attention.)* Folks ... Mrs. Palama and Mrs. Malama have been teaching the hula for a long time. "Holoholo Kaa" is just the beginning. Wait till you finish. Your dancing feet and swaying hips will be graceful when you leap around in the next one about a crazy princess ... Princess Pupule.

MR. SMITH

I hate to sound like I'm complaining, Pete, but when we all dance in these group lessons ... I can't see steering an imaginary steering wheel *(Demonstrates.)* ... well that takes care of my hands, but ... going up and down hills, around winding roads ... Well, dancing is not ... *(Gives up as the group laughs good-naturedly.)*

(The husband of the Southern couple gets up to demonstrate.)

HUSBAND

It's easy. You hold the wheel like this *(throws his arms forward stiffly)* and you let yourself go like this ... *(belly dances. Everybody laughs. The wife gets up and pulls her husband down.)*

PETE KAPIOLANI

Folks, you've been a wonderful group ever since you got off the plane and on to my bus. *(The group responds with cheers.)* Besides the hula, I want you to remember something about this ... *(waves to the cliffs and the audience.)* Captain Cook discovered the Hawaiian Islands, and it was here in Kealakekua Bay ... so long ago. 1779, he met a tragic end. It was a great loss to mankind. Remember, Cook lived in the days of sailing ships. In 1768 he explored the south seas ... that was in Tahiti, to set up scientific equipment to see the planet Venus for the Royal Society. Then he sailed around New Zealand and Australia ... he mapped 2,000 miles of Australia's east coast and claimed it for Britain. That was in 1770.

(The husband of the New England couple)

HUSBAND

In those days, you just went into a new territory and put a flag on a pole, just like in the United States, the British put their flag on our pole ...

(The husband of the Southern couple)

HUSBAND

But then in 1776, we signed the Declaration of Independence and said we ... don't want a British flag, we want our own American flag ...

PETE KAPIOLANI

And that's why every 4th of July we have fireworks. We commemorate the signing of the Declaration of Independence, July 4, 1776. It was about that same time that Captain Cook was preparing for his third voyage to the South Seas, July 1776. In 1772, his second voyage took him towards the bottom of the world, he was the first to circumnavigate the Antarctic Circle. He was extraordinary, to create maps wherever he went so other sailing ships could utilize them. By 1776 ... the Dutch, the Russian, the Spanish, the Portuguese navigators wanted a shorter route to link the Atlantic Ocean with the Pacific, and the British sent Captain Cook. That's when he discovered the island of Oahu, later Kauai, and Niihau. That was in 1778. He was able to refill his water casks, and supplies of fresh fruits, vegetables, chickens, goats, pigs ... and continue his expedition to the Northwest. It was on his way back in 1779, that he discovered Hawaii, and came into this famous bay.

MR. SMITH

And he put Hawaii on the map.

PETE KAPIOLANI

And he put Hawaii on the map, yes.

MRS. SMITH

Why did he meet a tragic end?

MR. SMITH

Mob violence. Whenever mobs of people gather, and you find it happening even today, a rock thrown, a pistol fired, someone gets hurt, and ... next thing you know so many are dead. Something excites people in a mob.

PETE KAPIOLANI

To understand the Hawaiians in 1778 ... you have to remember they had no written language, but were told, by word of mouth, that someday, Lono, their God of Plenty would return on a floating island. When Captain Cook arrived with his ship, broad sails flapping, like a mighty white bird, or floating island, he was worshipped as a God. The people prostrated themselves before him. He didn't understand the Hawaiian language ... and communication ... even today, a television age ... communicating to cultures unlike our own is important. *(The group look at each other and slap each other compatibly.)* Folks ... you can read about the details of Cook's death in books. Right now, I want to keep you all together so we can visit the site of the old temple, the Heiau. The old Hawaiians were superstitious, and they still believe that because Captain Cook was killed here and his bones buried somewhere, this place is haunted.

MRS. SMITH

This place is haunted?

PETE KAPIOLANI *(Laughing.)*

Not really, but it does keep my tourist groups together. Come on, follow me ...

MRS. SMITH

What if the bones were hidden in a temple, the Heiau?

JOE KALAMA

Oh don't worry. If you believe that place is haunted, you'd believe that everytime the volcano erupts, Pele, the Goddess of Fire is having a fit.

MR. SMITH

And nobody is that crazy. Although ... I'd rather take pictures of a volcano erupting ... Pele having a fit ... than taking pictures of us hula dancing.

PETE KAPIOLANI

Come on folks ... to the Heiau. *(Exits Pete UPSTAGE-LEFT, followed by respectfully silent people, except the Smiths. Joe Kalama strums a tune quietly on his ukelele as they disappear in the coconut grove. Mr. Smith walks DOWNSTAGE-RIGHT to take photographs.)*

MRS. SMITH

Come on dear ... we'll get lost, like the hula teachers, Mrs. Palama and Mrs. Malama.

MR. SMITH

Good, then we don't need to take the hula lessons.

MRS. SMITH

Please dear, this place is so ... silent ... *(laughs nervously.)*

10

MR. SMITH

We won't get lost. I've traveled all over South America, and I've heard all about Gods and Goddesses of the Mayas, the Aztecs, the Incas ... in fact the Incas in Peru, what's left on top of Machu Picchu, now that's worth photographing. Here ... just pose here. This is another of their old Gods, the God of War, Ku. *(Mary comes timidly and says "Hi!" to the post).* He's just a sign post, now, don't be nervous. Smile ...

(As Mr. Smith is photographing different angles of Mrs. Smith, Chiefess Kalehua enters UPSTAGE-RIGHT. She wears a red sequined, transparent holoku over a skin colored leotard. Maile strands decorate her head, and around her shoulders. She walks unnoticed between the Smiths as they are photographing.)

MRS. SMITH

Now you come here. I'll take your picture, dear. *(They trade places. Mr. Smith looks at the war God Ku, and mimics the glowering Ku. Chiefess Kalehua takes offense. She goes up and kicks his shins. Mr. Smith, like a slow motion camera, reaches down and rubs his shins.)* Don't move dear.

MR. SMITH

Sorry. For a moment ... *(He scratches and scratches his head, looks at the God Ku, then resumes a ferocious pose. Chiefess Kalehua kicks him in the seat of his pants. Again, like a slow motion camera, he reaches behind, rubs himself, then turns quickly to see who kicked him.)*

MRS. SMITH

Please dear, turn around.

MR. SMITH

Funny! I thought someone kicked my shins a minute ago, and ... just now ...as if someone kicked my behind. Do you believe this place is really haunted?

MRS. SMITH

Haunted? *(Nervously starts to call and run back and forth for Pete.)* Pete, wait up. Come on dear ...

MR. SMITH

Hold it, Mrs. Smith. *(Mrs. Smith calms down as Mr. Smith grabs her hands.)* People who believe in ghosts are crazy. So, calmly, let's find Pete. *(They walk calmly, then run UPSTAGE-LEFT and exit.)*

CHIEFESS KALEHUA *(sadly)*

Tourists ... everywhere, noisy tourists carving their initials on everything ...

(She walks to the thatched hut, STAGE-RIGHT, takes the calabash from the raffia holder, throws the vines and flowers down, sits and thumps unconsciously accompanying herself, her moods, just as a person today drums his fingernails while speaking to someone on the telephone. It is suggested that in order to create the rhythmic patterns on the calabash, that one refers to "Ancient Hawaiian Music," by Helen Heffron Roberts, Dover Publications, New York, 1967 for percussive ideas.)

CHIEFESS KALEHUA

(Talking calmly to herself while thumping on her cala-bash)

IF ONLY we could go backward ... just once ... enjoy the carefree past. Way, way´ back, 200 years ago. Who knows? *(Shrugs her shoulders and sighs.)* If my chief had lived ... not killed by a stray bullet, 200 years ago ... he might have become a greater warrior too, like the great, great Kamehameha. *(Sighs.)* Who knows? Oh, to be happy once again ... to laugh ... to feel like a bird ... like a fish to swim out to Captain Cook's sailing ship. *(Stops her thumping.)* Captain Cook ... I've seen you Captain Cook from up there *(Nods to the cliffs.)* You walk these shores still ... My chief was great only in my eyes. You, Captain Cook, were great in the eyes of the world. *(Sighs.)* If only we could go backwards ...

(Offstage, Pete Kapiolani's tape recorder is blasting "Hawaiian War Chant" with the malihinis participating with grunts and "auwes." Chiefess Kalehua sighs, then lies down and goes to sleep. Enter Pete Kapiolani UPSTAGE-LEFT with tape recorder, followed by an exuberant, exhilarating group of uninhibited tourists flapping their arms, hitting their thighs and feet. They are individual in their noises, but all keep following Pete over the hilly mound, around the thatched hut, and shout "Au we" during the chorus. At the end of this group marching, they flop around the rowboat, DOWNSTAGE-LEFT.)

13

PETE KAPIOLANI

Wasn't that fun, Mr. Smith?

MR. SMITH

That wasn't dancing, or was it? At this point, I'm ready to go "Holoholo Kaa" for some lunch. That kind of dancing makes me hungry.

PETE KAPIOLANI

We'll take the canoes down that way *(Waves to an exit in the audience.)* Our box lunches will be waiting for us near Captain Cook's monument. *(At the mention of Captain Cook, a disheveled, middle-aged, irascible ghost of Captain Cook stands in the rowboat and pantomimes anger. He is wearing body colored leotards and a transparent sequined night shirt. He puts on a wig, then a three cornered hat, a sword, holster belt hurriedly.)*

MR. SMITH

Pete ... this *(Knocks on it.)* is solid wood.

PETE KAPIOLANI

Yes, it's been here a long, long time, too. Mrs. Palama said it represents Captain Cook's boat, stolen off his ship the night before he was killed.

MR. SMITH

You don't say! A haunted rowboat.

PETE KAPIOLANI

The strange thing about oral stories and superstition is that people may say this boat is *not* haunted, but then, just in case ... they don't want to have anything to do with it.

MRS. SMITH

Do you suppose over there at Captain Cook's monument ... people say it's *not* haunted, but ...

MR. SMITH

Mary, Captain Cook lived some 200 odd years ago. If Captain Cook's ghost is still around, I'll shake hands with him. *(He goes about knocking the rim of the boat and Captain Cook tries to shake hands a couple times, then gives up trying.)*

PETE KAPIOLANI

Folks, there's time for snorkeling, collecting puka shells ... and of course, the famous Captain Cook Seafood platter in a box ... Fresh lobster/shrimp/crab salad. For you adventurous gourmets ... side dishes in a box of lomi-lomi salmon, fresh sea urchin, raw limpets, dried octopus and sour poi.

MR. SMITH

Two orders of Captain Cook's lobster/shrimp/crabs. *(Everybody in unison orders the same, except the man from Japan. In halting English, he exclaims he will try the dried octopus because he is in the Import-Export business, and his company sends dried octopus to Chinatown in San Francisco. General orders of one-inch pieces of the octopus by the group.)*

PETE KAPIOLANI

(Turning on tape recorder. Suggested music is "Aoia" sung by Nina from the record de Mello arr-Melway, Inc., Music of Polynesia, Inc.) Follow me, folks. *(Everyone exits after Pete humming happily and keeping time to the music offstage in the audience.)*

CAPTAIN COOK

(Sitting glumly in the rowboat). Tourists ... damn nuisance. *(Mimics Pete.)* Captain Cook's Seafood platter in a box. Well, I suppose I should be flattered to have a special seafood platter named after me. If I had stayed at home ... Yorkshire ... Yorkshire. Did I make a mistake leaving the land for the sea ... *(Contemplates. Lights dim. BLACKOUT and SPOTLIGHT UPSTAGE-CENTER. James Cook in his teens is bidding farewell to his parents and two brothers on a hill in Yorkshire, England. They wear clothing appropriate for the period, 1745.)*

YOUNG JAMES COOK

(With conch shell to his ears.)
I can hear the roar of the ocean, father. Here, you listen.

FATHER

(Irritably.) Damn nonsense. All this blathering about oceans in a seashell. Imagination. That's what. Plain, fool, imagination. Son, for the last time, reconsider ...

MOTHER

Father, please ... give him your blessing. Let the boy live by the sea. The sea comes natural to him ... from my side of the family.

FATHER

From my side of the family, he's a born farmer, a land lover. He plows a straight line, too.

MOTHER

But his heart is not here, in the land. It is the sea that calls to him. *(Starts to cry and is consoled by her husband.)*

1ST BROTHER

As an apprentice to a grocer ... what will you learn about the sea behind the counter?

2ND BROTHER

You'll be measuring sugar, weighing cheeses, salt herring, well, that's fish, salt herring ...

1ST BROTHER

When will you have time for the sea ... with running errands, sweeping the grocer's floor?

YOUNG COOK

I've never seen the sea. But Staithes is by the sea. At night ... I can go down to the ships and listen and learn. I can learn what it's like, the new world ... Crossing the ocean to settle in the new colonies, the far, far East, the ... undiscovered land. From the top of the mast, a sailor sees in the distance ... New Land ... *(Forgets himself.)* Ahoy-y-y there, new land ahead. Land ho-o-o! Land ... *(Mother sniffles louder.)*

FATHER

(Embraces son.) Son, you be a good apprentice to the grocer. He's already on land. God bless you!

MOTHER

God be with you son ... and bring you home safely to Yorkshire. *(The lights dim slowly as the brothers slap each other fondly and they all wave as Young Cook runs off the hill. BLACKOUT, then spotlight James Cook, in his twenties, DOWNSTAGE-RIGHT speaking to a British Admiral, vintage costumes 1759.)*

ADMIRAL

James Cook ... you have been highly recommended to me ... as an excellent sailing Master, knowledgeable about surveying, making maps. We are, as you know, at war with France. For years now, the French colonists in Canada have been fighting our own colonists. If we can remove France's foothold in the New World ... blockade France's reinforcements, supplies ... Well, well if we don't, the whole of Canada will be lost to England.

JAMES COOK

Yes sir!

ADMIRAL

The French Army is entrenched in Quebec. Our fighting ships cannot move on Quebec, because the French have destroyed all markers and buoys in the St. Lawrence River. They intend to stay. New soundings of the depths of the river must be made, charts drawn up. The job has to be done.

JAMES COOK

I shall do my best, sir.

ADMIRAL

Thank you, Cook. *(Paces for a moment.)* All this must be done only at night. The French are in league with the Indians. Those Indians have eyes like hawks.

JAMES COOK

I shall do my very best, sir. *(The Admiral looks at him gratefully. His tone of voice changes from an official to an informal tone.)*

ADMIRAL

Very good, Cook. I say there ... about your training in surveying, map making. You would have been younger than I at the Royal Academy of Science. You *did* study there, of course?

JAMES COOK

No Sir, I did not.

ADMIRAL

Indeed! Then what is your schooling?

JAMES COOK

Since I was thirteen ... I have been ... self-taught, sir.

ADMIRAL

Extraordinary! You are extraordinary, Cook. All success to you, Cook. Remember, the fate of every man aboard our fighting ships, depends on your mission. *(Both men salute. The Admiral steps out of the spotlight. Cook takes out a notebook, walks DOWNSTAGE-LEFT and looks up over the audience's head. Two seamen are standing near the rowboat waiting.)*

JAMES COOK

The stars. Thank God, for those stars. What would a sailor do without those guiding lights, moving in the celestial orbits. *(Chuckles.)* Must have been difficult for Copernicus to explain the same cluster of stars moving in their orbits. Difficult these days to communicate to people like the Admiral. *(Mimics.)* You would have been younger than I at the Royal Academy of Science. You *did* study there, of course? *(Laughs.)* I'm glad I didn't, because I like to work with my hands, as well as with my brains. *(He takes notes after looking at the stars. The two seamen shift their weight from one foot to the other.)*

1ST SEAMAN

Is Master Cook finished talking to the stars?

2ND SEAMAN

Aye, mate, he's almost.

1ST SEAMAN

What the devil do you mean ... almost?

2ND SEAMAN

Just that, almost! You can't study stars fast! Takes time!

1ST SEAMAN

(Cusses under his breath.) Okay, mate. Okay. It sure is hard to talk to you. Where I come from, everybody's friendly. (2nd Seaman becomes agitated and looks furtively around.) That's nice, to be among friends. Warm friends. On the street, in the pubs. There's no curtness. Even at the table, we say please and thank you. No hostility, where I come from. Only plain, honest folks. (2nd Seaman is beside himself and sh-h-h-h 1st. Seaman.) There you go again. You have no cause to get worried about being my friend. I won't say another word to you. I can take a hint. You don't want to talk to me.

2ND SEAMAN

Sorry. No offense. I didn't want those Indians to hear us.

1ST SEAMAN

What Indians?

2ND SEAMAN

Indians that scalp people, that's what. The French have Indian spies.

1ST SEAMAN

Indians that scalp people ...

2ND SEAMAN

And maybe not only our scalps, we'd lose, but our lives.

1ST SEAMAN

God almighty! Sh-h-h, don't talk so loud. *(Cook closes his book. All three get in the rowboat and sailors simulate rowing. Cook is in the rear and simulates throwing out a line with a weight. The lights dim slightly.)*

COOK

Br-r-r-r, the wind blows madly ... like the North Sea. Three days to chart the currents in this snarling river. We've worked hard, men. *(Suddenly, tom-toms are heard loud and clear. Both seamen frantically row.)* Easy now. Bear Starboard *(The lights get dimmer.)* Now get out and run ... run. *(The three get out. BLACKOUT. Then the ghost of Captain Cook gets up from the floor of the rowboat. He looks around for his wig, finds it, places it on his head, as well as his three cornered hat and climbs out of the rowboat. Offstage, he hears Mrs. Malama calling Mrs. Palama in a yodeling fashion. He goes UPSTAGE-CENTER and listens.)*

MRS. MALAMA

(Offstage.) Aine-e-e-e-e Hooey ... Elizabeth Palama. Wait for me!

COOK

(Sits dejected on the rocks.) Tourists, even up there.

MRS. MALAMA

(Offstage.) Elizabeth ... hoo---ey.

MRS. PALAMA

(Offstage.) I'm over heah! Come on. Slide down ...

COOK

Elizabeth Palama ... *(Sighs.)* ... Elizabeth. My Elizabeth. How patient you were all those years. How lonely it must have been to be a sailor's wife. My ship dropped anchor here, Elizabeth. *(Kalehua has awakened and is listening.)* I like to listen to the ocean breaking. It's quiet when the sun sets. If only I could have a cave of my own *(Looks up at the cliffs.)* ... away from the noisy tourists ... yes, way up high.

CHIEFESS KALEHUA

Captain Cook? Captain Cook?

COOK

What? Someone called me?

CHIEFESS KALEHUA

Yes. I called. I heard you speak about a cave of your own ... up high.

COOK

(Embarrassed.) Oh ... I'm so tired of noisy tourists. I was just talking to myself.

CHIEFESS KALEHUA

A cave of your own ... up high? *(Points to the cliffs.)*

COOK

Well yes, but ... I know that's the burial grounds, kapu. *(Stops suddenly.)* Whom am I speaking to?

CHIEFESS KALEHUA

I am called ... Kalehuaulaokekaioleleiwi. My chief calls me Kalehua for short.

COOK

That is a beautiful name. Kalehua.

CHIEFESS KALEHUA

Mahalo! You were saying ... *(Waves to the cliffs.)* ...

COOK

Oh, I was just talking to myself. You see, all my life I've found it hard to talk to people ... so, I have a ludicrous habit of speaking aloud ... to the stars in the night. An eccentricity, I suppose ...

CHIEFESS KALEHUA

I talk to myself all the time.

COOK

To yourself? You talk to yourself?

CHIEFESS KALEHUA

All the time. *(They both laugh.)* But ... talking to the stars, sometimes ... Only our Kahuna does that.

COOK

(Thinks for a moment.) Your Kahuna, the high priest, talks to the stars?

CHIEFESS KALEHUA

All the time.

COOK

Does he speak to anyone in particular, I mean does he have names of the stars he talks with?

CHIEFESS KALEHUA

He has names for all the stars. Hawaiian names for animals and people. I can't remember them all, but there's the God Maui, who keeps running across the sky, lassoing the sun ...

COOK

Lassoing the sun at night? *(They both laugh heartily.)* Well, I find it easy to talk to you. It would be very interesting to meet your high priest, your Kahuna.

KALEHUA

Yes, he will like you, too. We have watched you often from up there *(Waves to the cliffs.)* You always walk in sorrow when the tourists come to visit these shores.

COOK

(Angrily.) Tourists. Everywhere, tourists. *(Stops and apologizes.)* I'm sorry. These tourists will drive me insane.

KALEHUA

Yes, I know. Noisy tourists. I've learned a lot about the world just listening to the tourist guides and the tourists. They are noisy, yes, I know. Would you like a cave next to the Kahuna, our high priest?

COOK

Oh ... *(Thinks for a moment.)* ... I don't mean to impose.

KALEHUA

Oh, you will not impose. I shall ask my chief ...

COOK

(Excitedly.) Ask your chief?

KALEHUA

Yes ... ask my chief. After all, I am his favorite chiefess.

COOK

Favorite chiefess?

KALEHUA

Yes. There are eight of us, we all have our own caves.

COOK

Oh, this is ... *(Laughs.)* you know, a person must cultivate a sense of humor, or else he can't survive.

KALEHUA

A sense of humor?

COOK

Yes. A sense of humor. I mean ... do you suppose I could meet your chief and high priest and ... I can present my case, officially? I wouldn't want to break any taboos.

KALEHUA

(Excitedly.) Of course ... just as in the past ... just once more, we can have a ceremony for you. *(Claps her hands.)* Yes, just like in the past, 200 years ago ... with singing, feasting, dancing, sham wars ...

COOK

(Aghast.) Oh, I say ... I didn't want, I mean ... I do want perhaps a simple ceremony of greeting.

KALEHUA

Oh yes. I'll go right up and ... and ... and ...

COOK

Yes. And what?

KALEHUA

How will you speak in Hawaiian and ask my chief for a cave of your own?

COOK

True, true. How one communicates *is* important. Do you suppose *(Looks appraisingly at Kalehua.)* you could be my diplomatic emissary?

KALEHUA

A what?

COOK

(Takes a notebook from his person.) Oh, I must think and write this out.

KALEHUA

Are you writing a speech for me?

COOK

No, just step one, step two, and hopefully step three.

KALEHUA

Now you are talking like a man of action, step one, step two, step three. *(Puzzled.)* Are you going to dance?

COOK *(Laughing.)*

This is too much. *(Puts his notebook away.)* If I must, I shall communicate somehow ... as in the past, I shall enjoy your ceremony of welcome with chanting, dancing, and sham wars.

KALEHUA

I know my chief will like you. *(Offstage, Mrs. Malama is calling "Elizabeth Palama, aineeeee." Mrs. Palama answers "over here, Mary Malama").* The tourists' hula teachers! Quickly, to the Heiau! I shall pray to Pele to cover the trail to the caves. My chief will hear about this ... *(Exit UPSTAGE-LEFT, as a weary but laughing elderly Mrs. Palama enters UPSTAGE-RIGHT followed by a bedraggled Mrs. Malama.)*

MRS. MALAMA

Elizabeth Palama. The next time you take me for a hike, I want to see a road map. Oh my, I hurt all over *(Rubs her behind.)*

MRS. PALAMA

We made it down.

MRS. MALAMA

Yeah! You said ... one-half mile down!

MRS. PALAMA

I said straight down. We went on the kapakahi trail. The crooked way.

MRS. MALAMA

That trail must be for mountain goats!

MRS. PALAMA

(Leading the way to the thatched hut.) Here, lie on your opu. I'll give you a first class lomi-lomi. *(She pounds roughly and quickly on Mrs. Malama's back, that Mrs. Malama howls: "Pau, Pau.")* See, it works real fast, my lomi-lomi. A little hike is like jogging. Good for old folks, like us.

MRS. MALAMA

Speak for yourself. Next time I'm going holoholo kaa. You know Palama, you're *(Can't contain herself from laughing.)* ... coming down that cliff ... you're ...

MRS. PALAMA

I'm what? *(Flexes her muscles.)*

MRS. MALAMA

Good fun, even if you have funny ideas.

MRS. PALAMA

That's my friend talking. You know Malama, not many of my friends are left.

MRS. MALAMA

Yeah, and this is one friend you nearly lost on that cliff. Oh my, I nearly had a heart attack when there was no trail. *(Laughs.)* And it was no laughing matter, when I had to slide.

MRS. PALAMA

Yes, I guess I'm too old too, for that kind of hiking. You know ... when I was young I used to camp by Captain Cook's Monument, way over there. *(Waves at the audience.)* My kuku used to say, "See those caves up in the cliff, *(Points to the background.)* well, those caves are kapu. Our royal Hawaiian chiefs are hidden there." And I told her without thinking ... I said: "Kuku, I went into those caves. They are empty. The Museum in Hilo has all the mummies of the Royal Hawaiians under their glass cases." And you know what?

MRS. MALAMA

What?

MRS. PALAMA

She started to chant ... crying and chanting that I was a hupo, but a good hupo. She prayed, oh my. I didn't tell her the rest of my story.

MRS. MALAMA

What was the rest?

MRS. PALAMA

That I had gone hiking up that trail ... that same trail we came down ... only it was a little different. And I found a secret entrance ...

MRS. MALAMA

A what?

MRS. PALAMA

A small tunnel. *(Mrs. Malama looks more and more alarmed, and Mrs. Palama enjoys watching her friend's face.)*

MRS. MALAMA

It was the kapu tunnel?

MRS. PALAMA

Yeah! When I was young, I was brave, maybe stupid, as my grandmother called me, but good and brave, and fearless.

MRS. MALAMA

Then what did you do in the tunnel?

MRS. PALAMA

Oh, I crawled on my knees, too, and at a long distance away, I saw the blue sky, and so I kept on going. When I got to the end, I could look out from there. *(Thumbs to the caves in the cliffs.)* and see the whole Kona coast.

MRS. MALAMA

The whole Kona coast ... oh my, Elizabeth. That's where the kapu cave your grandmother said the royal bones were hidden?

MRS. PALAMA

Yeah, and then I remembered my kuku chanting prayers, and I said to myself. Maybe I better chant something, too. *(She takes the calabash which Kalehua had used. Starts to thump and think of something to say. Mrs. Malama gets very excited. She stands quickly and takes the second calabash hanging in the raffia holder.)*

MRS. MALAMA

My kuku always said, don't be afraid of ghosts. Just pray when you see one. I'm going to chant with you, Elizabeth Palama, just in case I stepped on some Kapu bones coming down that goat trail.

MRS. PALAMA

(Laughing at Mrs. Malama's nervousness.) Sh-h-h, just in case I offended any royal Hawaiian ghosts in the kapu caves, I sang "Kau Ka Hali'a I Ka." *(Mrs. Palama starts out chanting, and Mrs. Malama echoes her lines, so that somehow they sound like Madrigal singers. As they are chanting the lights dim slowly.)*

STAGE DIRECTIONS:

Enter UPSTAGE-RIGHT 4 drummers in transparent short red and yellow capes and malos to join the chanters in the thatched hut. They thump enthusiastically along.

Enter UPSTAGE-LEFT 8 hula dancers in transparent tapa printed sarongs. They carry their sticks, pebbles, calabash, uliuli and sit DOWNSTAGE-LEFT. They thump, too.

Enter UPSTAGE-RIGHT 16 modern-dancer-warriors with fluorescent torches wearing helmets, transparent short capes and malos. They circle the stage, then run over the rocky hill to wait for the entrance of the chief.

Enter UPSTAGE-RIGHT the Royal Hawaiian Chief with Kahili bearers and High Priest. The chief wears a simulated feathered cloak, malo, helmet with red and yellow sequins. The Priest has a shorter cape.

Enter UPSTAGE-LEFT Chiefess Kalehua followed by Captain Cook to meet the Hawaiian Chief on the mound. Chiefess Kalehua retreats to STAGE-LEFT, as the high priest gives a short feather cape to the Hawaiian Chief who in turn gives it to Captain Cook. Cook unbuckles his sword, holster, and gives those, as well as his three cornered hat in exchange. The Chief then leads the way across the mound, and sits with Cook UPSTAGE-CENTER.

(Mrs. Palama and Mrs. Malama's pseudo madrigal has come to an end. The drummers beat a few bars of music ... Mrs. Malama now starts to chant spontaneously speaking in English translation, just as naturally as Chiefess Kalehua spoke to herself while thumping on her calabash, "Na Lei O Hawaii" by Charles E. King. Refer to King's Book of Hawaiian Melodies, pub. Charles E. King, 1934.)

      Lovely is Hawaii, the island of Keawe
      Adorned with brilliant lehua and
      fragrant Maile of Panaewa.

Chiefess Kalehua approaches Captain Cook and lays a strand of Maile on his lap. She returns to STAGE-LEFT.

      Grand is Maui, with Haleakala
      And 'tis for thee alone
      The beauteous rose will e'er be sacred.

Enter UPSTAGE-RIGHT appropriate, transparent and sequined, 7 other chiefesses with appropriate flower or shell, or nut as in the past, a token of welcome to Captain Cook. The Chiefesses and all dancers will perform as if they were in a theatre in the round stage. Four Chiefesses will return to UPSTAGE-RIGHT, and thus the program of ancient Hawaiian hulas and sham war begins: Drummers introduction for 8 beats of music ...

1. Poli 'ahu *(The dance with sticks.)* by dancers ... *(Drummers continuity for 8 beats.)* ...

2. Pu'u onioni *(The dance with pebbles.)* by dancers ... *(Drummers give a long drum roll.)* ...

3. Ia 'oe E Ka La *(The dance with the calabash.)* by Mrs. Palama and Mrs. Malama, who accompany the dancers wildly, as well as authentically ... *(Drummers continuity, this time softer, gently)* ...

4. E Liliu E *(A commemoration dance to Queen Liliueokalani.)* by the eight chiefesses ...*(Drummers continuity for 8 beats)*...

5. Wahine Holo Lio *(The dance with the uliulis.)* group ... *(Finale sham war loud drum beats.)* ...

6. Sham War *(It is suggested that trained modern dancers engage in pantomimed battle of attacking, retreating, engaging, disengaging with appropriate falls and recovery. The fluorescent torches are used as spears, or clubs, never leaving the hands, all in pretense.)*

(Suddenly, there is a loud rumble sound offstage, and a percussive bang on a kettle drum. Flashes of red lights light up the smoking Kilauea in the background. The performers stop and cower at the sides, as the tourists, and Pete enter one by one, screaming "Pele ... the volcano ... it is erupting ... Let's go ... Pete ..." The lights come up brighter, and the tourists keep running and jumping and running over the mound. Captain Cook is so irate, he stands and waves his hands angrily at the tourists who pass him. Chiefess Kalehua goes up to him, takes his hand, leads him back to his seat and they seemingly have a private discussion. Chiefess Kalehua returns to her place, and Captain Cook and the Chief look as if they are enjoying the tourists.)

PETE KAPIOLANI

(Shaking Mrs. Palama and Mrs. Malama who appear to be asleep.) Wake up! Wake up! The volcano has erupted.

MRS. PALAMA

What! Where am I? Pele ... Auwe no hoi e.

MRS. MALAMA

Oh my, I dreamed we were chanting and dancing with our ipus. Oh my! What's happening?

PETE KAPIOLANI

Some of the folks are still missing. Here, *(Gives Mrs. Palama his recorder.)* Hold this. Everybody, listen ... Stay here together, I have to go back and hurry those bird watchers and Antonio and Fife. Please, stay together, then ... holoholo Kaa to the Volcano.

MRS. PALAMA

Holoholo Kaa ... okay everybody, your hula lesson.

MR. SMITH

Not now, Mrs. Palama. We'll take a rain check.

MRS. PALAMA *(Authoritatively.)*

No, Mr. Smith. As soon as we step on the gas here, we can holoholo kaa. *(She turns the music on the tape recorder: Holoholo Kaa. Everybody stays where they are, hold an imaginary wheel in their two hands and vamp right, vamp left, overexaggerating their hips and counting aloud one two three four, or one two three toe, or step step step together, while Mrs. Malama goes about helping and encouraging everybody. Mrs. Palama interprets literally, going for a car ride, the wind is blowing, going downhill, uphill, around the hill, step on the gas ...).*

About the time the group has been performing for a few minutes, enter the birdwatchers and Antonio and Fife, also Pete carrying snorkeling gear. Mrs. Palama pounces on them and they stand and steer the car and wiggle with the rest of the group. The Ghostly entourage laugh silently. Before the end of the song, Mrs. Palama announces Holoholo ... holoholo ... and they exit DOWN-STAGE-RIGHT. Joe exits strumming.

The Royal Hawaiian Chief stands and beckons for Captain Cook to come along. Both walk congenially towards UPSTAGE-RIGHT. The dancers, the drummers prostrate themselves, the warriors stand at attention as the entourage passes, and the curtain falls.

THE END

ON BEING A HERMIT

(A radio fantasy)

CAST

Reg Smith—elderly professor
Nora Smith—housewife
Maxwell—middle-aged school teacher
Opal—middle-aged school teacher
Blake—young school teacher
Students—teenagers: Toni, April, Sally, John, Brad, and
   Jack

Setting: An imaginary site somewhere in the hills in
California, 1980.

SOUND: BIRDS SINGING IN THE FOREST UP ... AND OUT

REG: (Walking then stops.) We're almost there, Nora! Smell that clean, fresh air. (Sniffs appreciatively.) Nora? (Yells.) NORA-A-A! Where are you?

NORA: (Cupping her hands.) I'm coming, Reg! This is ridiculous. Grown people playing hermits. Year in, year out. Same place. Miles from nowhere.

REG: I thought you were behind me?

NORA: I was. This hill is like a mountain. Oh-h-h my aching backpack! I rested a little.

REG: We're almost there.

NORA: Good! I can't make it faster.

REG: (Sniffs audibly.) Smell the pines ... the cedars ... the laurel leaves!

NORA: You smell. I've gotta catch my breath. (Takes deep breaths.)

REG: I'm smelling! I'm a different person up here. I can laugh at the world. (Laughs.)

NORA: (Slaps self.) I itch all over. Why do the flies bother me, not you?

REG: I can laugh at myself up here. Cuss my enemies. Damn you computer freaks! Hah! (Laughs.)

NORA: When you're happy, I'm happy. That's me. Simple minded. (Sighs.) This kind of trek is too much for me. It's no vacation. No electricity in that rickety cabin. No running water. (Slaps self.) Only insects.

SOUND: BIRDS SINGING IN THE DISTANCE UP ... AND OUT

REG: The birds are ... symphonic.

NORA: We have birds in our yard. Quails, pigeons, brown towhees, orioles, doves, mockingbirds, hummingbirds...

REG: These are different birds.

NORA: Chirping robins, cheep-cheep sparrows, camp robber jays. Did you bring the insect repellent?

REG: In my backpack.

NORA: (Walking and slapping herself.) How far is it to that cabin?

REG: (Walking in place slowly.) Around this bend. There, Mrs. Smith. The sign. (Laughs.) Keep Off! Private Property. Trespassers will be prosecuted. Hm-m-m.

NORA: This is such a lonely place. Why don't we pitch a tent on Mt. Shasta? Then we'd see the landscape for miles. We'd be away from everybody.

REG: A skull and crossbones might be menacing. What did you say, Nora?

NORA: I said, too bad we can't be on Mt. Shasta. It's higher than this hill.

REG: Yeah! I need to practice drawing. Why not a skull and crossbones? (Laughs happily.)

NORA: You sound happy.

REG: I'm happy, happy, happy.

NORA: If these trees make you happy, why don't you plant trees in our yard? Sugar pine, Monterey pine, Scotch pine, cedars, you name it, the nursery has it. Blue spruce, green spruce, Douglas fir ...

REG: It's not the same. It's not the same.

NORA: Not the same birds. Not the same trees. I'm beginning to sound like a broken record.

REG: There, Mrs. Smith. Home at last. I'll ... unlock the door, swing it open and wait a second.

SOUND: SEVERAL CLICKETY CLICKS, DOOR CREAKS OPEN SLOWLY, THEN POTS AND PANS RATTLE NOISILY.

REG: Ha! My burglar alarm worked.

NORA: May I have the insect repellent, please.

REG: An intruder would've been knocked unconscious. Bang! Right on the noggin. Serve him right, for trespassing.

NORA: Reg, the insect repellent.

REG: Okay, okay! (He slaps his pockets and searches.) Here, Mrs. Smith. Something tells me you're irritated.

NORA: Irritated, hah! If you heard what I was saying about insects ... hiking, hiking up, up, and away from folks, maybe you'll understand my frustration. (Rubs self mumbling noisily.)

REG: Whenever you're unhappy you argue.

NORA: Argue? This insect repellent eases my pain. The insect bites. (Rubs self noisily.) Rub a dub dub, three men in a tub.

REG: Don't get hysterical. We can leave, if you like. Nobody to stop us. Leave any time.

NORA: Oh Reg. I'm sorry. Please smell the trees. Listen to your birds. If we must play hermits, okay. No sweat.

REG: (Walks a few steps.) Nothing disturbed. (Sniffs.) A bit moldy. A little cobwebby.

NORA: Chase the spiders!

REG: I'll chase 'em. Look at the scenery!

NORA: I'm looking. Miles and miles of treetops.

REG: Look up there!

NORA: A bald eagle?

REG: A red-tailed hawk. Isn't it beautiful? Gliding. Circling. Maybe it saw a rat ... hawks can, you know. So peaceful ... then zoom, there it goes. Like a dive bomber. Aren't you glad you're here? Oh, never mind. The deer will come to stare. You like the deer.

NORA: I like the deer. I don't trust the ugly black bears.

REG: Harmless black bears. We've never had to use the shotgun like the old hermit. "Shoot over their heads!" That's what he said. He knew how to take care of 'em. The bears knew. He did it once. They learned. (Recites.) Quote Poe's raven, Never More.

NORA: Nice to have that shotgun, just in case. The hermit must have had a rapport with bears.

REG: That shotgun isn't the best. A good yell and a SHOO! works better. You know, I can spend the rest of my life as a recluse. Recluse ... not one of those back-to-nature freaks.

NORA: No? What kind, then?

REG: A recluse in a comfortable setting. Maybe ... like those computerized asses who don't give a damn. They get paid plenty. Stupid freaks!

NORA: Great! Then I can look forward to indoor plumbing, electricity. But there's no people here. Nobody to talk, to share a cup of coffee.

REG: (Angrily.) People ... You don't have to go out in this world to compete, to´be aggressive. It's a dog's world out there. Gr-r-r-r!

NORA: Yes, dear, I know. More women are going out of the homes to yip-p-p-p! I like yapping at home. I can think creatively at home. Clip recipes. Try 'em out.

REG: You're like your father, trying out recipes.

NORA: Escargot with garlic sauce.

REG: Phew!

NORA: Messy cheese sauce on steamed clams.

REG: I'm glad restaurants serve finger bowls to wash up afterwards.

NORA: Raw starfish ... that's sea urchins. Tastes delicious, sweeter than raw oysters.

REG: Ugh! Food ... plain food. I'm starved! I hope you brought some plain, palatable fare.

NORA: Mom is like you. She squirmed at inky squid. She helped my father with his gourmet dishes.

REG: Who wouldn't squirm?

NORA: Everybody!

REG: Everybody who?

NORA: Everybody who likes gourmet food. Look at Pepperpot! It's black pigs feet, pigs ears, pigs tails...

REG: So what! So...squid looks inky in Spain or Portugal, and it looks like pink curled soft macaroni in some other country. And...and pig trotters look pitch black in pepperpot, and white bones in gelatin somewhere else. Sure, what the food looks like...me and your mother squirm. After all, we're not everybody, we're somebody. Namely your kin. My palate is my palate. It tells my stomach a few things. And I'm sure your mother's stomach talks to her, too.

NORA: (Laughing.) Okay, okay. Do you know...dad used to pick fresh herbs for curry recipes when we lived in India? After his lectures at the University, he'd gather fresh herbs with some of the local people. He ground his own spices.

REG: Ha! I'm like your mother. Never mind picking herbs. Get 'em in a box, it looks sanitary. No wonder your mother never liked curries. Your father's gourmet recipes.

NORA: (Giggles.) Well, he was...a hot curry fixer. I'll need your burglar alarm...the pot, not the frying pan...so I can cook some plain soup, not too spicy with herbs from a box.

REG: Now you're being creative. (Kisses her.) I'll start the woodstove.

SOUND: POTS JANGLE AS DOOR SQUEAKS AND CLOSES. NEARBY, BIRDS ARE TWITTERING, UP ... AND OUT.

MAX: (Walking slowly.) That boarded cabin must be close. I saw it flying over. Not easy, finding it on foot. Maybe ... I should've parachuted markers. No ... maybe this field trip for the kids will end up ... No! No! Max ... Think positive! Okay, now I gotta face facts. Can't hike all day. I hope Opal hurries up. I gotta tell her. I think we're lost in this forest. (Slaps self.) Damn mosquitoes. If my old man was alive, he'd say: "Max, keep away from forests ... no lights. You'll get lost. You're a city boy. (Chuckles.) Yeah Pa. I never got lost in New York City. Look at me now. This is a crazy world, Pa. What am I? A broken-down old school teacher. All these years in the teaching profession ... I end up in a boarding school, broken-down school for rich, dum-dum kids. Maybe, I should've stayed in your garage ... earned a decent living with grease in my ears. But I learned about cars from you, Pa. Funny thing ...

44

nowadays, kids like grease in their ears. I help the kids fix their broken-down cars. (Laughs.) You never saw such junk, Pa. They must make special field trips for junk parts. I know they wanna take off somewhere, split ... bum around, just live for now. The kids are good kids. Maybe mixed up ... parents too busy to raise 'em, or split up parents. Kids! Oh my God! I forgot about 'em. I hope Blake is jogging with 'em in the right direction. Maybe they'll find that cabin before we do. (Calls.) Opal. Opal-l-l-l. (Shouts.) OPAL-L-L!

OPAL: Yoo-hoo, Maxwell!

MAX: You okay?

OPAL: I'm okay!

MAX: Good! Take your time. (Slaps self vigorously.) If some good comes from this field trip, I'm reading about birds and bird whistles. I can't tell the difference between mockingbirds and warblers, but mockingbirds imitate other birds. Smart Alecs! (Reads.) Woodpeckers. Woodpeckers can cling to vertical trunks, propped by stiff tail feathers. Hm-m-m, stiff tail feathers. It pecks for food, peck, peck, peck ... food. I'm getting hungry sitting here. I hope we find that cabin soon, so we can eat.

SOUND: DISHES RATTLING AND SOUP IS BEING STIRRED.

NORA: (Giggling happily.) Watched pots never boil, Reg.

REG: Want me to stir?

NORA: No thanks! I'm not complaining, but this isn't quite like my electric stove, my microwave oven. But the wood smells good. Makes the room cozy. If only...

REG: Only what?

NORA: Oh ... just a thought.

REG: What thought?

NORA: Well ... if there was some electricity ... maybe some of those solar heating panels ... that's just a thought.

REG: This is a pseudo log cabin. Built for pioneers.

NORA: Pioneers. Wagon-wheels. No car pollution and stuff.

REG: The notched wood for the walls and roof, that's an art. A lost art. Very practical for the hermit before us, and for ourselves. Keeps us from the elements ... animals. The wood stove is our heat. The smoke drives the spiders out. (Laughs.)

NORA: Funny, funny.

REG: This is no different from India ... out in the villages. They didn't have microwave ovens or electricity. They had cookstoves, cow dung fuel. The women swept their dirt floors immaculately with tree branches. They carried well water in jugs on their heads. They were happy in villages.

NORA: I suppose ... they made something out of bare necessities. If we didn't do the same, like jumping in our car and leaving our comfortable house in Calcutta with all the servants, just to get away from people, we'd miss seeing village people.

REG: Whose idea was it to jump in and drive into the unknown, to keep going from Calcutta to Darjeeling?

NORA: (Laughs.) Well, we always had enough road maps. It was fun!

REG: Your idea ... driving our tiny car. By airplane, it would've been a vacation. By car, I almost had a heart attack, several of 'em.

NORA: (Dramatically.) We had two ... whole ... weeks, glorious weeks of adventure. (Snaps irritably.) We didn't hike, hike, hike ...

REG: We had to cross five rivers.

NORA: (Giggles.) At least my idea resulted in a change of scenery, of people. We observed village life styles, didn't we? We saw tea plantations, acres of lichee nuts. We rode those raft-ferries. That was exciting. Almost like riding the rapids. Remember?

REG: How could I forget. Every time I see a river now, I remember. I even remember that beautiful bridge which spanned the Ganges. The dirt ramps weren't finished ... but we drove over. We found roads. With the raft-ferries, we never made it across to the road on the other side. The current was always so strong.

NORA: One of the ferries reminded me of Venice.

REG: Venice?

NORA: Old Venice ... with gondoliers poling. And the song, O Solo Mio.

REG: Old Venice?

NORA: (Laughs.) You have to shut your eyes and imagine. It was funny, anyway. We drove our little car on the raft-ferry, then twenty or more pedestrians got on, then an ox and cart drove on, and ... the gondolier shoved off with his pole.

REG: (Laughs.) It's funny now, but at that time, that bullock started lowing and kicking. I never thought we'd make it across, but we did. Not straight across. The current took us miles away from the roads on my road map.

NORA: You know what?

REG: What?

NORA: I think we are, what we are ... with the people we've met not only in India, but in South America, Europe, Asia, Middle East, Africa ... Just meeting 'em, talking to 'em, even if there's a language barrier ... we change. We grow and become different, or indifferent, inside and outside ...

REG: Is the soup ready? I can hardly wait for something to change my insides.

NORA: (Laughing.) Coming up, one bowl of nutritious plain soup with special herbs from a box.

REG: Thank you Mrs. Smith. (Recites.) Ah, why do I love you? Let me count the ways ... after my soup.

NORA: Elizabeth Barrett Browning would have recited her poem before eating, but never mind.

REG: Ah! Good plain soup!

SOUND: BIRDS TWITTERING IN THE FOREST, UP ... AND OUT.

MAX: I guess if I didn't take time to read, I'd be skin diving, flying over the cabin ... (Sighs.) That cabin. It seemed a short distance from the highway where we parked ... east for couple miles, up and down the hills ... just a little north of Mt. Shasta ... Oh boy, what a mess we're in. Blake hiking with the kids. Rendezvousing at the cabin. What an idea. All my fault ... (Sighs.) May as well educate myself. (Reads.) The ring-necked pheasant: This Asiatic bird was introduced in the West ... found over much of the United States. It is a favorite game bird of farmlands, where it feeds on waste grain, occasionally causing local crop damage. Hah! I saw some of you today. Wish I had my shotgun. (Reads.) Western Quail have some kind of plume on their heads. What do you know ... another game bird. Now ... here's something for you, Pa. Pigeon. Pigeons are descendants of the wild Rock Dove of Europe. Though handsome birds, their nesting habits make 'em undesirables in cities. Well ... how about that? And the cooing of your pigeons, Pa, on our roof on the lower Eastside of Manhattan. All your racing Homers, the show breeds — Kings, Tumblers, Nuns and Show Flights. Undesirables on our roof. (Laughs.) I guess if we didn't do something to amuse ourselves, besides earning a living, we may as well be dead. Pardon the expression, Pa? You know something, when we were young? They used to call us mumblers at school. (Chuckles.) We mumbled when the teacher called on us. Ha! Let me tell you, Pa, I got a whole school of 'em, only we call 'em, slow ... learners. (Laughs.) B.F. Skinner and you, Pa ... both of you belong in the same ball park. Mr. Skinner taught his pigeons to play ping-pong. You taught yours to CRASH and CAPTURE enemy pigeons, the undesirables belonging to our neighbor on the next roof.

OPAL: Maxwell! MAX-X-X-WELL!

MAX: Over here, Opal.

OPAL: Hi Max! For a moment I lost my bearings. The trees and bushes looked alike. I thought I'd lost you.

MAX: I've lost my bearings, too, Opal. I can't figure out where I am.

OPAL: Let's find Blake and the kids. It's a good thing we just have six joggers. If we don't get back to the school, they'll send out search parties. It was a good idea to have Blake scout ahead. The kids have so much energy to burn. Good kids! Blake's a good teacher. (Both walk in their places.) Let's think positive, Max. (They laugh.)

SOUND: BIRDS TWITTERING IN THE DISTANCE, UP ... AND OUT. WATER IS POURED OVER RATTLING DISHES.

REG: Well, that's that. An electric dishwasher is faster.

NORA: A little piece of pipe to the tank outside ... Maybe a hole in the wall so we'd have running water. I'm sure the pioneers would have thought of it. You know ... I think we're too old to play pioneer games.

REG: Not too old to have pioneer spirits.

NORA: No ... not too old to have pioneer spirits. But I need practice to hike with pioneer gusto. Why won't you walk eighteen holes on the golf course?

REG: Don't start that again. I don't like golf.

NORA: Golfers are sociable.

REG: I know. I don't qualify.

NORA: It's a game ... which depends on oneself. Lots of singles join complete strangers teeing off.

REG: I like minding my own business. I don't like complete strangers. I can't be jovial over nothing.

NORA: It's a skill game. It challenges the mind. Requires total concentration. Then after you concentrate, you can be sociable.

REG: I like the idea of drawing and painting, like Winston Churchill. Total concentration sitting down. He started painting when he was forty. Kept at it for thirty or more years. Maybe I can ... call this my Art studio to concentrate.

NORA: President Eisenhower had an Art studio for him to sit in...in the White House. (Sighs.) I suppose I could write poetry while you paint, like Emily Dickinson. She was a recluse.

REG: A nice recluse.

NORA: In her own house. A poet doesn't need to have a cabin in the woods, miles from anywhere.

REG: Do you like Tagore?

NORA: The Hindu poet? Yes. He wrote beautifully.

REG: Sir Rabindranath Tagore. He was knighted by the Queen of England.

NORA: We had pioneer spirits when we were in his country.

REG: Whenever I get a whiff of sandalwood, I think of the bazaars ... hassling over prices. Strange, how memories are computed in one's brains. When I lecture in my classes, my sense of smell interacts automatically. A student's perfume drifts by ... fresh scents of soap, and poof! I'm transported to this cabin and smell the woodstove burning pine needles. I'm lecturing, yet, I'm far away ...

NORA: My brains are far out ... I hear musical sounds. (Laughs.) Your brain must have a good smelling input. Mine seems like a pipe organ. Any sound I hear, musical sounds, and my pipe organ vibrations react. Feels good. I'm transported to far off countries, those places where I heard strange sounds.

REG: (Angrily.) Computers. Computer freaks. How can they feed computers statistics ... cold hard facts, without human values. Working out mathematical models to solve economic problems ... without understanding complex, human values.

NORA: Don't get angry, dear.

REG: Then they pretend they're soothsayers.

NORA: You work so hard in money and banking.

REG: Worthless models. Idiot instructors. Worst part of it ... the students like the computer freaks. Bah!

NORA: Listen to the birds, Reg. Smell the pines.

SOUND: BIRDS TWITTERING UP ... AND OUT.

HIKERS: (Walking until hearing the word freeze) Hep, one two, one two.

BLAKE: Halt! HALT! HALT! That means FREEZE! (A noise persists.)

BRAD: Sorry. I had to move. I had to scratch. (Scratches self.)

BLAKE: Next time ... when I say something, do it! You hear me?

ALL: Yes Sir! Yes Mr. Blake! Yes, Yes, Yes.

TONI: We've been jogging and jogging, Mr. Blake. Where's the cabin?

APRIL: Are we lost, Mr. Blake?

BLAKE: Of course not, April. We're not lost. Not totally.

JOHN: Let's not go around in any more circles. I'm pooped.

BRAD: We could send smoke signals to tell people we're safe. (All giggle.)

JACK: Yeah! Hey Brad, that's a good idea! Maybe people are looking for us, even if we're not lost.

SALLY: The ranger could see the smoke.

BRAD: Then they'll send a helicopter. (Makes noises like a chopper.)

TONI: Yeh! (Panic.) Over here! We're down here! Throw a rope! (Cries dramatically.) Oh ... sav-v-v-v-e us!

SALLY: I'll go up first. (*Brad:* No you don't. My idea. Me first. *John:* I'm after Brad. *Jack:* I'm next after John.) No you don't. (Slaps them; they slap back.)

APRIL: (Sniffling.) When's my turn?

BLAKE: Hold it! Hold it! (The kids quit slapping each other.) This is no time for charades. Don't think about smoke signals. Just sit! Stay put. I'll scout for ... five, ten minutes. Okay? Hey, where're you going ... Brad, John, Jack? (*Boys:* Gotta go, teacher. Gotta...)

BLAKE: (Angrily.) Come back fast, you guys! Darn it. That leaves you girls alone. You're not afraid to sit and wait? The boys'll be back in a second.

TONI: We'll sit and wait, Mr. Blake. We're not afraid.

BLAKE: I'll scout around. Easier to scout alone. I'll be back in five ... ten minutes, no longer.

APRIL: Find Maxwell fast, Mr. Blake. I'm starved.

BLAKE: Sure, sure, April. Take care, Sally, Toni.

SALLY: Don't worry, April. Max's dependable.

TONI: Yeah! He means well ... even when he yells. Teaching John, Jack, Brad is no picnic. They don't hear unless you yell.

SALLY: They haven't grown up. They don't want to grow up. That's why Brad makes so much noise. He still wants to be a baby ... to imitate noises.

TONI: John's handsome, but dumb.

APRIL: Jack's not too smart, but I'm the dumbest. (April laughs at herself. *Sally and Toni:* Oh no, April.)

JOHN: Yah-h-h-h! Ugh! Phew!

TONI: What's the matter you guys?

JACK: (Laughing.) John's dancing. Disco dancing.

BRAD: He stepped on some p-p-p-p-t-t-t-t-t! (Laughs.)

SALLY: Don't scare us. Bad enough we're lost, although Mr. Blake won't admit it. We gotta keep cool. Calm.

JACK: That was deer p-p-p-p-p-t-t-t-t-t!

JOHN: Deer? Huh? More like an elephant.

BRAD: Elephant? No elephants here. Maybe grizzlies, like Grizzly Adams' pet on TV.

APRIL: Maybe whatever it is ... is still around. I wish Maxwell was here. He can do anything. He fished me out of the kelp bed at the beach last month.

JACK: Max is nice to you, you're a girl. When I got tangled in the kelp, he just yelled: Get out! Get out! Don't just stand there! You wanna drown?

SALLY: I untangled myself in the kelp. Nobody needs to tell me what to do. I like finding out how to solve problems. Everybody has to grow up and solve problems.

JACK: (Sarcastically.) You don't say! I solved my problem. I didn't drown. Hah!

JOHN: Max is a first class mechanic. He knows his carburetors.

BRAD: Yeah! When he yells: "Follow the diagrams, can't you read?" he's mad, hooey-y-y-y!

JACK: Pretty hard taking the carburetor apart, then putting it back ... so many pieces to remember.

APRIL: I'm a slow learner. I don't think yelling helps me learn faster.

JACK: Well ... you don't need to work on carburetors. I gotta. When I put a car together, my dad's gonna give me a Jaguar. He's a car dealer. He's got one in his showcase.

JOHN: My dad says he ain't buying me nothing. If I can build a car from scratch, he promises to insure it. He's an insurance agent. He gave mom a Cadillac. She split. Left us.

BRAD: If I had a car, any kind that goes, I'd split, too. That's what a car is for. (Makes noises of car shifting gears and driving away.)

APRIL: My folks have a motorhome. They want to see all of the United States.

TONI: My folks want to see the world by plane, boat, train ...

SALLY: Our folks are too busy for us. We gotta fend for ourselves. As soon as I pass my driving test, I'm taking off.

APRIL: I can pass the driving test, but I can't drive.

BRAD: How the hell can anybody pass tests? I flunk 'em. I can't read. Maybe I need glasses. Naw! I'm going to race cars when I grow up. Just drive round and round. (Makes noises of driving a racing car.)

JACK: I can read diagrams. They should have more pictures in the driving tests.

TONI: Yeah. I can drive. I keep flunking the written test. I gotta pass. I don't wanna get old and ride the plane, boat, train. I wanna drive myself.

SALLY: How do you pass, April?

APRIL: It's easy.

ALL: EASY!

APRIL: Yeah! I memorize a word with a ... ah ... picture. Or is it a question with a word? Maxwell says, do both ways. Just come out with the right answers on the paper. And it works!

ALL: What works?

APRIL: When you read the questions slowly, you remember the picture or the word. It's like a special code in your brain. You put it in yourself.

BRAD: I buy that ... read slowly. I can't read fast, anyway. I dunno that picture stuff. Sounds spooky.

JACK: Is a diagram a picture?

SALLY: Brain ... we got a lot of coding to do. We gotta do something.

TONI: I Gotta try. I dunno how, yet.

JOHN: Crazy game. When I build a car from scratch, I'll think about it.

APRIL: What do I do about driving ... it's not easy.

BRAD: Take it easy. Don't roar the engine. That makes Max nervous.

APRIL: That's all? Take it easy. Don't roar the engine?

SALLY: Some people need more physical practice ... practice makes perfect. It takes time to learn to coordinate ... to drive a car. You have to keep trying. You'll get it. Max is a good teacher.

APRIL: I gotta be mobile ... and not make Max nervous.

BRAD: Yeah, April. Easy does it. (Shifts gears slowly and carefully and drives off smoothly.)

APRIL: There I go ... down the street, all by myself. (Laughs.)

SALLY: (Suddenly.) Sh-h-h-h! Did you hear that?

APRIL: Hear what?

JOHN: I smell ... something.

SALLY: Like a grunt or a sneeze ...

BRAD: I didn't hear anything.

JACK: I didn't hear anything.

SALLY: Sh-h-h-h.

APRIL: (Whispers.) What is it?

SALLY: (Whispers.) Don't know. Maybe it was my imagination. I get jumpy when I feel I'm lost. I begin to hear things.

JACK: (Whispers.) Maybe we better find Blake.

SALLY: It was like a twig snapping, then a grunt, like a pig.

JOHN: Aw Sally! The forest's full of chipmunks jumping ... (Sniffs.) I smell something.

SALLY: Did you step on something? Maybe that animal is back.

JACK: Maybe we better find Blake.

APRIL: I think I'm getting nervous.

SALLY: If we have to run, April, I'll hold your hand.

APRIL: Thanks, Sally. I can't run fast.

TONI: (Laughs.) Look ... you cutie thing!

ALL: Where, where?

TONI: A bear cub. Under the bush. Over there! See? Come here cutie!

SALLY: Oh my goodness! Don't touch it! The mama will tear you apart.

JOHN: Yeah! Outta my way. I'm splitting! (Runs.)

JACK: Quit shoving, John. (Runs.)

BRAD: Hey you guys! Wait for me! (Runs.)

GIRLS: (Running in panic.) BLAKE-E-E-E! E-E-E ... O-O-O-O-O...

BLAKE: Hey! What's up? Wait for me! Don't ... Oh what's the use. Imbeciles. Can't leave 'em for a minute, and they're in trouble. Can't teach 'em anything. Opal spoonfeeds 'em. Max yells. Not me! Either they discipline themselves, or else ... I'm splitting. Can't waste my time teaching dum-dums. (Thinks.) Another school, maybe? Other kids? Hm-m-m. Couple years of this, and I'll be off my rocker. I need some kind of ... interest. Max flies. Yeah! He gets away for couple hours. Flies by himself, crop dusting for his friend. Maybe I could ask him if ... if ... I could go along. Maybe I could parachute out. Just drift down by myself. Naw! That wouldn't work. I don't like being alone ... (Yells.) I'm coming. Hey! Well ... I ... I think, oh my! A cub! Yow! It wants to play. Shoo! Shoo! It's coming after me. O-O-O-O. (Runs.)

SOUND: BIRDS TWITTERING IN THE DISTANCE, UP ... OUT.

OPAL: Oh, that was close. I thought I'd never make it up the tree. Thanks, Max! I can see the cabin from my perch. It's close. That-a-way, leftside when we make a dash for it.

MAX: Maybe, if I throw more pine cones at it ... there! take that! and that! Shoo! Shoo! Go way!

OPAL: What if it doesn't go away?

MAX: We'll stay treed. (Laughs.)

OPAL: This is no time for jokes, Maxwell!

MAX: Sorry Opal. What a day! Not only lost ... now we're held captive.

OPAL: I wish I had one of those belts for lumberjacks. My arms ache.

MAX: Come down a bit.

OPAL: How far down? I don't dare look.

MAX: Come down about ten feet. Shimmy.

OPAL: What?

MAX: Shimmy ... never mind. Put one leg down, lower the arm, squeeze the trunk, do the other side ... got it?

OPAL: Got what?

MAX: Think of an inchworm backing up ... only back downwards.

OPAL: Inchworm? Back up, only downwards? I'll try. I never thought I could climb up a tree ... oh dear! Oh-h-h!

MAX: Good! Good! You're doing fine ...

OPAL: This is an undignified descent, but I'm not too old to try. Ugh! Oh!

MAX: (Laughing.) There. It wasn't difficult. There's space for the two of us to sit on the branch. A bit snug, but safe.

OPAL: (Laughing.) Always a first time. I've always had a fear of heights, but when that bear stood up, I forgot everything. You were wonderful to give me a hoist. Whew!

MAX: Too bad I didn't throw our backpacks up. We could have our picnic lunch now. I always wanted a tree-house, like pigeons.

OPAL: Oh, that was a scare. Not only that brute, below, but coming down ... my heart's pumping, oh!

MAX: Bears don't attack, unless the mama has a cub. I read somewhere ... mama kangaroos often drop their young in the tall grass when they sense roo hunters. Then they bong-g-g off and lead the hunters away from baby. A merry chase. Afterwards, the mama comes back to the exact spot in the high grass, and baby hops aboard. Real service.

OPAL: I hope this mama goes off to find her cub. Look! She's tearing our backpacks.

MAX: Oh, no. There goes our lunches. What a day! Nothing going for us. We may as well find the kids and Blake ... head home. I hope we can find our bus. (Sighs.) If only I had saved our lunches ...

SOUND: TINKLING OF SPOON STIRRING TEA.

NORA: Nice ... having a cup of tea. Being here with your special birds outside. Good idea. The wood stove makes it cozy in here.

REG: I'm glad you're coming around to enjoying the cabin. This is what I need. Some time to think. To get away from people. The generation gap is sad. I don't know what happened. I was young ... then suddenly, I'm too old.

NORA: You're an excellent professor.

REG: Thanks. I need compliments.

NORA: The subject matter may be ... a little difficult.

REG: Money and Banking? Difficult? No. Can't be. It's easy being objective, analytical, factual ... nothing to it. It's like any subject. It's difficult if you don't learn the vocabulary. Students are so fascinated with machines ... and younger instructors with mathematical models to fit the machines ... that they fall asleep in class. I've taught the same courses in universities ... all over the world. You can tell when you communicate. Students ask questions because they want to learn something from you. Keeps one alert. Stimulating! Am I getting to you, what I'm saying?

NORA: (Laughs.) I haven't fallen asleep. You gotta keep going, Reg. It's like playing golf. It's your game. Only you ... can perfect it.

REG: Is that all you can think of? A golf game?

NORA: If you learn to play golf, you'd know what I was talking about. We'd have a common vocabulary. Right now ... you know you have to put the little ball in a hole and hit it with a club to do it. That's a start. But ... the actual performance, the feeling of concentration, of hitting the tiny, iddy biddy ball so it lands right where you want it, that is a skill only the performer ... controls.

REG: Hm-m-m. You've communicated something. Yet, I'm not sure I know what it is. I get it. Yet, I'm not sure I got it.

NORA: Have another cup of tea. (Shouts.) Hey! Look! People!

REG: Wha-wha-what?

NORA: Out there! Kids running. Six of 'em. Wow! They're coming here! They're running, holding hands, falling over each other! They must be playing a game.

REG: (Belligerently.) This is private property! They can't trespass!

NORA: Maybe they're lost?

REG: It's invasion of privacy. They can't get lost on my property.

NORA: What can we do?

REG: Show 'em the way down.

NORA: Oh, please Reg. Couldn't we ask them in?

REG: Absolutely not. I forbid it. This is my private hideaway. I need the time to myself, to ourselves. Time to think!

NORA: Maybe they're hungry. Or thirsty. We're kind to people at home.

REG: That's different. That's home. This is my private place.

SOUND: FRANTIC KNOCKING FOLLOWED BY FISTS POUNDING.

NORA: What shall we do?

REG: Go tell 'em how to get back on the trail. Tell 'em anything.

NORA: You go!

REG: You always talk to people. You go!

NORA: I can't shoo! people.

KIDS: (Screaming and crying.) HURRY! HURRY!

REG: (Shouting.) Okay, Okay!

SOUND: DOOR OPENS SQUEAKILY.

ALL: Bear! Shut the door! Shut the door!

SOUND: DOOR SLAMS SHUT. TABLE, CHAIR, DISHES CRASH TO THE FLOOR.

BRAD: Yuk-k-k-k. Soup all over me.
REG: (Angrily.) What's the big idea ... crashing in here. Where's your manners?
APRIL: (Sniffling.) There's a bear outside ... we were so scared.
SALLY: We're sorry we crashed in. We ran and ran.
APRIL: (Crying softly.) And we fell down ...
REG: Don't cry, young lady. Don't cry. I'll shoo! the bear.
JACK: It was only a cub.
NORA: A cub? And the mama?
TONI: That's it! We thought the mama would tear us apart.
APRIL: It was terrible. I didn't think I could mobilize so fast. Can we stay inside here? We didn't wait for Blake.
REG: Blake? Who's he?
JOHN: Our PE teacher. He's a jogger.
SALLY: He's young. He teaches us math ... how to balance a checkbook.
TONI: He teaches drama. Shakespeare: "Tarry a little ... this bond doth give thee no blood; the words—a pound of flesh," Portia was smart.
BRAD: Yeah! We play charades all the time. That's the new way of teaching, Blake says. Works on rats and pigeons.
APRIL: Sometimes, he teaches us folk dancing, that's PE.
JACK: Yeah! I can't dance. Disco dancing, folk dancing. I'm clumsy.
REG: Mr. Blake must be a versatile teacher.
JOHN: He's okay. Max is better.
REG: Max? Is he outside?
TONI: With Opal. They're our old teachers.
NORA: Oh, this is delightful company.

REG: Nora, I'm glad you are delighted ... but what are you all doing up in the woods?

BRAD: Field trip. Mr. Blake wanted to jog. And Max said he knew about a deserted cabin. He flew over it, whoosh ... like "One Flew Over the Cuckoo's Nest." (Laughs.)

JOHN: He said we could have a picnic lunch here. We hiked ahead of 'em.

JACK: He's a super teacher. He does things. He flies, goes scuba diving. And he teaches us how to take cars apart.

APRIL: One of these days, Max will teach me how to drive. He teaches Driver's Ed.

JOHN: Yeah! He yells, but he don't mean nothing.

REG: (Authoritatively.) Doesn't mean nothing ... I mean anything. You do have someone teach you English, speech classes?

JOHN: Opal. She teaches proper nouns, proper this, proper that ... no bathroom graffiti. (Boys guffaw; girls snicker.)

TONI: You'll like her when you meet Opal. She's our house mother.

APRIL: She's prim and proper. I'm gonna be like her.

JOHN: An old maid?

SALLY: (Slapping John.) Don't be stupid.

JOHN: Okay, okay. You don't have to be violent, Sally, hah!

REG: (Clearing his throat.) I'll look forward to meeting Opal, Max and Mr. Blake. Now ... who are you? We haven't been formally introduced.

APRIL: I'm April. (*Sally:* I'm Sally. *Toni:* Toni, short for Antoinette.)

BRAD: I'm Brad. Shall I shake hands, sir?

REG: (Laughs.) Men do. Good to know you Brad. And you?

JOHN: How do you do, sir, I'm John.

JACK: I'm Jack.

REG: This is Mrs. Smith. I'm Mr. Smith. Now that we are familiar with names, will you ... all, pick up the broken dishes and tidy up this mess.

ALL: (Laughing happily.) Yes Sir!

REG: (Aside.) They paid attention, Nora! Look at 'em tidy up!

SOUND: UNNECESSARY BANGING OF FURNITURE BEING RIGHTED AND DISHES BEING THROWN PIECE BY PIECE INTO THE GARBAGE BIN.

APRIL: (Whispers.) Mrs. Smith ... ah ... is there a restroom?

NORA: (Whispers.) Outside, April. Turn left and walk twenty-five steps.

APRIL: (Laughs.) Oh! I hope Max comes soon. He can do anything.

BRAD: (Shouts.) Hey! Look! Mr. Blake! The cub!

ALL: Where? Where? (They laugh and shout.) Run! Run! (Brad sounds a make-believe bugle call at the horse races.)

REG: I never saw anything like that. The cub wants to play.

NORA: It's following Blake like a kitten. (Giggling.) It's tumbling, oh-h-h. Like a ball of black angora.

BRAD: Open the door! Hee, hee, hee!

JOHN: Run, run! Ho, ho, ho. (Girls clap; boys whistle.)

ALL: HURRY! HURRY! ha, ha, ha ...

SOUND: DOOR OPENS SUDDENLY FOR A SECOND THEN SLAMS SHUT.

ALL: You made it, Mr. Blake! (They clap and laugh.)

BLAKE: Oh-h-h-h. That dumb bear. We zigzagged ... oh-h-h-h!

APRIL: Are you okay, Mr. Blake?

BLAKE: Yes, April. Only pooped. I never ... oh-h-h-h.

REG: (Clearing his throat.) How do you do!

SALLY: Mr. Blake ... let me introduce you to Mr. Smith.

BLAKE: How do you do! Excuse my entrance. I was scared. I saw the cabin ... the door was open. I ran in. Thanks!

TONI: And this is Mrs. Smith, Mr. Blake.

BLAKE: How do you do, Mrs. Smith. I'm sorry for ... intruding.

NORA: (Happily.) Oh, I love ... unexpected callers. I'm very happy to meet you, Mr. Blake.

BLAKE: One more field trip like this, and I've had it. Goodbye Ranchero.

REG: That's your ranch-school?

BLAKE: Yeah, you can call it that. A few nags for the kids. I can't stand the beasts. Where's Max ... Opal?

REG: Outside. I don't remember seeing any schools nearby?

BLAKE: Oh ... we're hundred miles south. Max likes hundred mile field trips ... east, north, south, west, up in the air, under the water. Hah! I'll have ulcers before my time. Hey you kids ... WHY didn't you stay put?

JOHN: We was frozen ... we were frozen. You told us to freeze. We did!

BRAD: Then we smelled the cub, John did, and Toni saw it under the bush ... We split.

JACK: Yeah! We called you. Didya hear us?

APRIL: I mobilized.

SALLY: We ran and ran. We didn't stop yelling and running.

TONI: We stayed together, Mr. Blake, like you told us ...

REG: (Chuckling.) Apparently, you have rapport with your students.

BLAKE: Rapport? (Laughs.) Do I have rapport with you kids?

JOHN: What's that ... rapport?

JACK: My dad and I have rapport. He says: Knock on wood (Knocks on his forehead.) all the time. He's gonna give me a Jaguar when I put car parts together, knock on wood. (Knocks on his forehead.)

JOHN: That's rapport? Well ... my dad and me, my dad and I have rapport. He said make your car from scratch, I'll insure it. Rap on your port. (Knocks on his forehead.)

BRAD: I never see my dad. He's a jet pilot. (Whooshes like an airplane taking off.)

TONI: Nothing to talk about to my folks ... they said I belong to another generation, something like that.

SALLY: I don't have rapport ... well-l-l-l, maybe when I'm with my dad. But not when I'm with my step-dad.

APRIL: My folks are always traveling, so ... I don't have rapport.

REG: (Chuckles.) So much for rapport. I had harmonious rapport in mind ...

BLAKE: (Laughs.) Everybody's tuned in on a different frequency.

SALLY: Shall we wait for Opal and Max, Mr. Blake?

BRAD: Maybe we can make smoke signals on the roof. I'll climb and put a blanket over the chimney, then whoosh, whoosh, whoosh, that makes smoke signals.

BLAKE: NO SMOKE SIGNALS! Put your thinking cap on. There's a dumb cub outside.

APRIL: Did you mean we can't climb the roof?

BLAKE: Hm-m-m-m. I didn't say don't. Why the roof? Why not a tall tree, it's higher? This is a forest, isn't it? Lots of tall, straight trees.

SALLY: Hey Mr. Blake! That's a brilliant idea.

BLAKE: What is?

SALLY: Climbing a tree. I climbed a redwood when I was lost once. My dad found me.

BRAD: Hey ... I wanna do that! (*Jack:* Me too! *John:* Yeah! Me three!)

BLAKE: HOLD IT EVERYBODY! Nobody climbs without permission. Think, think ... whatcha do about that dumb cub?

REG: Let me make a suggestion.

BLAKE: Mr. Smith has a suggestion.

REG: A good shoo! and a shout will do the trick.

NORA: Oh Reg-g-g-g ...

BLAKE: Are you sure ... I mean, ah, that cub didn't pay any attention to me.

REG: Then that's settled. I'll SHOO! SHOUT! Just wait here.

SOUND: DOOR OPENS SLOWLY, SLAMS SHUT, THEN FOOTSTEPS RUNNING, UP ... AND OUT.

TONI: Look! Three bears.

NORA: Reg-g-g-g! Oh-h-h-h. Where's Mr..Smith?

ALL: (Panic stricken.) Oh, oh, oh ...

BLAKE: Three bears! Now, I'm getting mad. Where's the broom?

NORA: Broom? What for?

BLAKE: Whack 'em! Teach those beasties a lesson!

NORA: We have a shotgun!

BLAKE: (Horrified.) Oh! I don't wanna kill 'em!

NORA: Scare 'em! Shoot over their heads!

BLAKE: Shoot a gun? I've never shot a gun!

SALLY: I'll do it, Mr. Blake. Please! I can shoot a rifle. I've shot ducks with my dad! Please!

BLAKE: No you don't Sally!

SALLY: Then you shoot! Scare the bears!

BLAKE: (Positively.) Sure! Show me!

SALLY: Here ... it's loaded. Cock it! Aim ... and pull this, that's the trigger.

BLAKE: Cock ... aim ... pull this? That's all?

SALLY: I can do it, Mr. Blake. Please? Please?

BLAKE: No! Cock ... aim ... pull this. Open the door!

SOUND: DOOR OPENS QUICKLY ... SLAMS SHUT. SHOTGUN ECHOES.

ALL: (Clapping excitedly.) Hurray! Hurray! Blake did it.

NORA: Reg? Where's Mr. Smith?

BRAD: (Scuffling with others.) I'll climb the redwood. (*Jack:* I'll climb. *John:* I'm gonna climb. *Sally:* Get off my foot John. *April:* The bears! Look! running off. *Toni:* Ladies first-t-t.)

SOUND: DOOR OPENS AND BANGS UNNECESSAR-ILY.

NORA: Reg-g-g-g? REG-G-G?

REG: (Shouting.) MAX-X-X-X-X! OP-P-P-AL-L-L!

NORA: Whatcha doing up that tree? Oh-h-h! Be careful. You'll fall! Mr. Blake! Mr. Blake! Mr. Blake!

BLAKE: Ow-w-w-w my shoulder! oh-h-h.

SALLY: You did it, Mr. Blake. You did it. You shot the gun. The bears ran.

BLAKE: What happened, my arm feels funny?

SALLY: You didn't brace yourself. You know. Brace. Guns kick ...

BLAKE: Oh-h-h ...

SALLY: I have some horse liniment ...

BLAKE: (Horrified.) Oh my God! What's Mr. Smith doing up there!

NORA: Mr. Blake! Mr. Blake! Do something!

BLAKE: We need a ladder! A ladder! Hey you guys! Brad ... John, Jack. Get down! Get down! Oh what's the use ...

BOYS: MAX-X-X-X! O-O-O-PAL! (*Girls:* Max, hi! Opal-l-l!)

MAX: Hey Mr. Blake! Hi Girls. Hey you guys! DOWN!

OPAL: (Laughing and crying.) Hi Mr. Blake, girls ... (Shouts.) Oh, Max. Do something! Do something! Look! The giant redwood!

NORA: Hang on! Don't fall! Oh-h-h-h ...

MAX: We ... just got down a smaller tree. Can I help? (*Reg:* YESSSS!)

BLAKE: We need a ladder. A ladder!

NORA: We don't have a ladder!

BRAD: Why don't we make a ladder, like in the circus?

MAX: Ladder. Like circus acrobats?

BLAKE: Human pyramid?

NORA: Oh-h-h-h ... and everybody tumbles? Reg can't tumble.

SALLY: It's easy! Tuck your chin and roll, Mr. Smith.

REG: Hell! Do something. I'll curl up ... make the ladder.

MAX: (Authoritatively.) Okay. We make a ladder. Jack, Blake, me on the bottom rung ... Brad, John, get up on our shoulders. (Scuffling sounds; *Brad:* I get up like ... don't move Jack ... ah, oop. *John:* Hard to get up-p-p on people ... oop. *Blake:* Ow-w-w-w my shoulder, easy John. *Brad:* I better take off my shoes. *Jack:* Phew! You stink John. *Max:* Get up Brad before I black your eyes. *Brad:* I getting up, I get-t-t-ing there. There! I got Mr. Smith's foot. Whatta I do? *Blake:* Hold it! *John:* I got the other foot. I'm holding!) Okay-y-y Mr. Smith. Work your way down the rungs.

NORA: Be careful, Reg. (*Opal:* Inch down. I made it down. You can.)

SOUND: WHOOSH AND THUMP LIKE A TREE FALLING.

NORA: (Laughing and crying.) Oh Reg. (*Girls* clap and giggle.)

REG: What happened?

SALLY: You tucked and rolled like a professional.

MAX: That was a ... ah, eh, hum-m creative ladder. And it worked! Ha! Good idea, Brad. (Slaps him.) Couldn't work without you guys, knock on wood, John, Jack. (Knocks on their foreheads.) Quick thinking! Now we can go home. Hep, one two, one two ...

GIRLS: (Fussing.) Home? *April:* I'm starved. When do we eat? *Sally:* I wanna shoot the gun! *Toni:* I'm hungry.

BOYS: (Fussing.) *Brad:* We came here to eat! *John:* We walked and walked, now I wanna eat. *Jack:* Where's the food? You promised!

MAX: Wow! Look at this museum piece. Whatta shotgun!

SALLY: Mr. Blake shot over the bears. Scared 'em. Can I shoot it, Max? Please. Just once. Please, please, please ...

MAX: No, Sally. Hey, Blake. Maybe we can go hunting sometime?

BLAKE: That gun kicks ... ah ... yeah, Max. Maybe, sometime ... that would be nice. I gotta practice bracing. (Chuckles.)

OPAL: Girls, the bear ripped ... the backpacks. (*Girls:* Horrified: Oh-h-h!) Ate our food. We're sorry we have to go home.

MAX: (Authoritatively.) Okay boys ... girls ... (*All:* sadly: Oh-h-h-h.)

NORA: I have some plain soup? (*All:* Yum-m-m!)

OPAL: Oh thank you, but we must be going. (*All:* Oh-h-h-h-h-h-h!)

REG: We haven't formally met, Max, Opal, but you have a bunch of swell kids. Innovative. Like circus people. (*Max, Opal:* proudly: Yes-s-s!)

NORA: It was nice meeting you Max, Opal. You must come again.

BLAKE: If Max and I go hunting ... sometime, we'll drop by and say hello.

REG: (Chuckles.) My wife ... and I, will be happy to share some hot soup, not too spicy with herbs from a box. That's my wife's special gourmet soup. Goodbye, Mr. Blake. Opal. Max. Boys. Girls.

SOUND: BIRDS TWITTERING IN THE DISTANCE.

ALL: (Walking slowly away.) Goodbye ... goodbye ...
(*Opal:* Listen to birds whistling, girls. *Max:* Warblers ..
remember that word, boys.)
NORA: The birds ... do sound different, don't they Reg.
Reg: Yes. (Kisses her.)

SOUND: BIRDS TWITTERING UP ... AND OUT.

ON LOVE AND MARRIAGES

(A Closet Play)

ACT I

ACT II

CHARACTERS

SAM uninhibited shoeshiner-cobbler

MIKE conscientious newsvendor-proprietor

LORNA the Masons' pretty cook-maid

MATILDA the Turners' robust cook-maid

MRS. TURNER attractive widow; Chad's mother

CHAD youthful, unaffected Artist with a beard

PROF. MASON dignified, balding widower; Terry's father

TERRY beautiful nineteen-year-old women's liberator

OTHERS MODERN DANCERS for "people" scenes in Act I, scene 1 and 3; Act II, scene 1. "People" with lines are two police officers—one female, one male; two delivery men; two models—Lena and Rita

ACT I
Scene 1

The Scene:

This is an imaginary intersection of a hilly neighborhood in San Francisco. High rising condominiums have dwarfed two white stucco houses which face each other. Each house has a manicured lawn, bay window over the garage and reminds one of the Spanish architecture of townhouses in the city of San Francisco years ago. *Stage-right,* a sign over the door reads: The Masons'-Service Entrance. *Stage-left,* a sign reads: The Turners'-Service/Entrance to Art Gallery. *Downstage-center* is a boarded kiosk.

Stage Directions:

Imagine a city awakening. It is six a.m. People silently go to work, to golf, to jog in their own fashion. Two police officers saunter amicably. They exchange friendly greetings as Sam and Mike enter *stage right.* Sam and Mike open their kiosk. One end is Sam's Shoe business and people going to work silently and appreciatively get their clothes whisked and shoes shined. The other end is Mike's pulp store. People buy the morning paper. Everybody seems to know Sam and Mike. Then there's a lull, and Sam takes out his cobbler's tools and Mike busies himself displaying his comic books and fashion magazines.

(Enter Milkman, *stage-left.*)

SAM   Hiya Will! How's yore person-n-nalized shoppin biz. Bankrupt yet?

WILL   Hey there, Sam, Mike! (Sighs.) No. Not bankrupt, knock on wood. Only pooped. I'm not young no more. What a hill! Whew!

SAM   Whatcha got? A whole dairy?

MIKE   Where you going?

WILL   The Masons'. Oh, my aching back. My sore feet. These hills get steeper each year, I swear. I gotta quit running errands. Hard on my gizzard, or whatever I have.

SAM   You sure gotta lot of chicken eggs anyway, my, my.

WILL   They must be expecting a lot of company for dessert. I got enough eggs, butter, whip cream, ice cream, half 'n' half, low-fat cheese, and Terry said she wanted jumbo strawberries and alfalfa tea.

SAM   Wow! Dat's sure dairy products even to de tea bags.

MIKE   They must be having crepe suzettes for the wedding breakfast. Isn't that nice.

SAM   Crepes?

MIKE   Yeah. You know. The thin pancakes.

SAM   You don't say. Lorna told me she had to cook breakfast for fifty. Crepes? I hope there's some leftovers when I visit Lorna.

WILL   Is Professor Mason getting married?

MIKE   No, not him. Terry. She and Chad, tomorrow. It's about time. They've been neighbors a long time, can't remember exactly. Nice.

WILL   Well, I'll be darned. Terry getting married. She's a fussy one. Never satisfied. For a young chick, she sure acts like an old hen. Well I gotta go, before she starts cackling. (Sam and Mike laugh as Will exits to the Masons' doorway, *stage-right.*)

MIKE   Nice, getting married in your own house. Less expensive. And Lorna cooking and cleaning up. No caterers. Nice. Like my own wedding, long ago.

SAM   Got married in yore house?

MIKE   Yep! Way back when ... Wapato. Good old Indian country, what's left of it anyway. It was apple blossom time. We ... Meg and I ... were right out of high school. No job. No nothing. That's the thing about being young.

SAM   Yeah! Nuts!

MIKE   (Laughs.) Nutty but imaginative. Full of love of life.

SAM   Sure. Den wat happened? Yore folks? Her folks?

MIKE   My folks? We were a close family. I had to tell 'em we planned to elope. Not those exact words, but after the yelling, my folks came around to see the great side of our story. We loved each other.

SAM   So you got married in yore house!

MIKE   (Proudly.) Yep! Of course we didn't have crepes, but a simple buffet—venison, wild duck, smoked salmon. Those simple everyday home-baked breads, five tiered cake and ice cream. My mom's fancy cooking and stuff.

SAM   I guess Meg's folks muss like you and yore Mom's cooking.

MIKE   Well ... Meg's folks, they never forgave us. Even after thirty years, ten grandchildren and two great grandchildren.

SAM   Boy! Dey muss be angry bout someting.

MIKE   Me. They didn't think I'd amount to anybody.

SAM   And look at you today ... a self-made proprietor.

MIKE	Yeah, not too bad. At least everybody in the neighborhood thinks so. But not my in-laws. Meg was an only child. Her father was a civil engineer.
SAM	Civil engineer.
MIKE	Yeah. He builds bridges and roads and stuff like that.
SAM	You don't say. Civil engineer.
MIKE	I guess my folks were farm folks, and I was a disappointment to him. Sometimes I wish Meg's folks would get used to me. Her mom is nice. Do you know that Meg's great-great-grandfather was an Indian chief on her mother's side?
SAM	Wow! A movie pitcher chief?
MIKE	No, a real one.
SAM	Wow! Meg has one drop of Indian blood. Meg don't look Indian.
MIKE	Her folks look like plain white people, too. Now ... my friend Manuel, he's Indian. Yakima Indian. He looks Indian.
SAM	Manuel?
MIKE	Yeah. He was my best man at my wedding.
SAM	Manuel? Dat's an Indian name?
MIKE	I think his father came from Mexico. His mother was a Yakima Indian. Manuel and I ... we used to go fishing for salmon every year when it went up river to spawn.
SAM	Yeah! Fishing. Mebbe de only nice sport I like in my hometown ... in de everglades of Florida ... is fishing. Catfishing. Good eating catfish. I used to ketch 'em wid stink meat. Jest dat smell used to knock 'em wild. You use a boat for salmon fishing?
MIKE	Well, you see, Manuel is an Indian. He can fish like his forebears in the state of Washington.
SAM	Forebears?

MIKE	Yeah. Like his father ... grandfather anyway, and uncles. That's the law. Indians can fish as they used to with spears and nets after the fish goes up stream.
SAM	Spear? You used a spear?
MIKE	No. I couldn't. Only Indians can use 'em. Manuel was very good at spear fishing. He caught enough for his folks and for me.
SAM	Wat you use for bait?
MIKE	(Sighs.) Herring. I'd cast out with my herring but the salmon didn't bite. Sometimes, I'd catch a bullhead. That's a kind of bottom fish, full of bones and a big head.

(Enter Milkman from Mason's doorway, *stage-right*. He seems upset and mumbles to himself incoherently as he exits hurriedly *stage-left*.)

SAM	Will ... muss have forgotten, or mebbe Terry sed someting to make him mad. (Seriously.) Now, dat Terry and Chad?
MIKE	They're young. Terry has good qualities. Good experience running her house for her old man after her mother passed away.
SAM	She's bossy, Lorna sez.
MIKE	Not really bossy. She's a typical teenager. She's nineteen.
SAM	You calls it de way you sees it. She's still bossy, and who wants a bossy wife?
MIKE	She's a normal, nineteen play acting a house-keeper. After all her father is a professor of drama. So ... why not be dramatic in telling Lorna what to do in the house?
SAM	Mebbe Chad is lucky and unlucky. Terry is good lookin', but bossy.
MIKE	Chad is imaginative, full of life. He has talent as an Artist. Not everybody can sketch criminals in court like him.
SAM	You don't need talent to handle Terry. Whoever heard of talking to a mule wid a paintbrush.

(Both laugh. Enter *stage-right* two police officers who exchange friendly greetings then exit *stage-left*.)

MIKE	Chad and Terry will make out. They love each other. Love makes the difference.
SAM	Hey ... I taught of someting.
MIKE	Yeah? What?
SAM	Wat if ... wat if Chad's mudder, who is a (Uses thumbs to indicate houses *stage-left* for the Turners' and then the Masons', *stage-right*.) ... a widow, and Terry's father, who is a widderer got marrid, too, den ...
MIKE	Good lord!
SAM	Den, (Uses his head to indicate houses.) Terry ken come over and liv wid Chad in one house, and Chad's mudder can move in wid Professor Mason in Terry's house.
MIKE	(Thinks.) That would take care of the housing problem. Mrs. Turner is pretty. She wears old fashioned dresses ... like stage costumes, so she and Professor Mason will have something in common to talk about when she tells him about her clothes. And Professor Mason, well, eh? Naw! It wouldn't work. He ain't interested. Whatever put that idea in your head? Man, you gotta grow up, leave your everglade background. You gotta get sophisticated. Professor Mason and Mrs. Turner, goodness, what a misfit. Crazy idea!
SAM	(Laughing.) I saw an ole movie lass night at de Oakland Museum. Lorna and me laughed ourselves silly. Mickey Rooney had horns on his head. His name was Puck. And Joe E. Brown was a transvestite. He wore a tutu. And James Cagney had an ass's head ...
MIKE	Hold it! What's those people got to do with Mrs. Turner and Professor Mason?

SAM   I'm coming to dat. You see, it was very funny, dat ole movie. Puck, dat was Mickey Rooney, got magic potions all mixed up wid wrong luvbirds ... but in de end, ev'rybody got straighten'd out. De misfit luvbirds had a double weddin'. De ferry King marrid de ferry Queen. And ... James Cagney's ass's head came off.

MIKE   Okay, okay. I get the picture. So you got the idea of the double wedding for the young love birds, that's Chad and Terry, and the old folks, Mrs. Turner and Professor Mason. (Thinks.) Kinda ridiculous. And I don't think any love potion will work on the old birds.

(Enter Whiskeyman *stage-right* with alcoholic beverages.)

SAM   Hey! Hello dere! Mebbe a double scotch on de rocks is better.

MAN   (Reads his delivery sheet.) Chad Turner.

SAM   Hey, dat's for Chad? I know him.

MAN   Know where he lives?

SAM   (Points to the Turners', *stage-left*.) My, my! Muss be a celebration over dere.

MAN   Lot of fire water! Thanks! (Exits *stage-left*.)

SAM   You're welcum. Didja hear him, Mike? Fire water. Dat means Chad must be having a stag party. Lass one before de weddin'.

MIKE   How about you, Sam? Ever think of you and Lorna settling down?

SAM   Lorna? How cum you pair me wid Lorna? She belongs to de Masons' house. De party is cross de street at de Turners'.

MIKE   (Thinks.) What? You mean ... you and Matilda are chummy?

SAM   (Laughs.) Right now, I'm percolating for dat lov-v-vable, curvay-y-yshush hunk of Matilda in de Turners' kitchen.

MIKE	Oh, Sam. You must be kidding? You and Matilda? What happened ... I mean, I thought Lorna and you. (Shakes his head.) I give up.
SAM	(Laughs.) I'm a bad, bad man. A loss soul. No use you prayin' for me. I'm gonna go to hell.
MIKE	(Irritated.) It's not right, Sam. Not right when you turn your love on and off like a faucet. Love means respect. The good with bad times, love is there.
SAM	Wat's de harm lovin' lotsa females? I'm good company. No complaints.
MIKE	Okay, okay. But .. isn't it confusing when you're in bed ...?
SAM	Hey, who sed anyting 'bout gettin' in bed?
MIKE	(Apologetic.) Sorry. I mean, when you're sleeping alone or with somebody. What I mean, doesn't your conscience bother you, two-timing somebody who is not there?
SAM	(Guffaws and gets up to demonstrate karate kicks and yells to an invisible conscience.) Ain't got no conscience. Long time ago, in de Everglades in Florida, I tole it, ain't no use you hangin' 'round. Shoo! (Kicks and chops his hands, hauls something imaginary over his shoulder and yells!) I mean it, shoo! (Sits and smiles innocently.) Ain't found my conscience since.
MIKE	(Thinks.) I give up. There's no hope for you without a conscience, but ... I'll quit praying. I'll tell Meg to quit. (Sighs.) But aren't there ... complications? Don't any of 'em, your girlfriends, get jealous of each other?
SAM	(Laughs.) De trouble wid you happily marrid men is dat you loss yore imagination. You ain't got no sense of humor left. (Continues to work humming merrily while Mike looks defeated.)

MIKE	Seriously, Sam. When will you settle down, with whomever?
SAM	Me? Settle down? I'm too young. Can't do dat when I'm still in my prime. Gotta keep moving, spreading my charms around.
MIKE	Time goes by fast. Don't you get tired being a bachelor?
SAM	I got marrid once.
MIKE	You didn't tell me.
SAM	I was nineteen. I was nuts and didn't have yore imagination.
MIKE	Nineteen? You said you left your Everglades when you were nineteen. Hitched rides cross country to San Francisco. (Thinks.) You're kidding, married at nineteen.
SAM	Well we was, then we wasn't, the story of my life.
MIKE	That kind of complication?
SAM	Yeah. Wen I looked down de rifle barrel, I said, hey man, we're marrid. Take dat gun away. Might go off!
MIKE	That was in her home? Got married?
SAM	Her home. Or her brudder's home. Or de one wid de rifle home. I dunno. I got to thinking. Sam, I sez, you too young to be saddled wid a wife. Dat was afta I karate kicked my conscience, so I was talkin' to de devil.
MIKE	(Thinks.) What a life!
SAM	So de devil sez, split you dumhead ... and dat's how I come here. (Laughs.) Ain't never goin' back.
MIKE	What happened to the man with the rifle? Or your wife?
SAM	Dunno, but ever since dat, I'm careful who I take out. Lorna's fun. No in-laws wid artillery. (Sam laughs. Mike shakes his head.) Me and Lorna ... we get along fine. (Enter whiskeyman from the Turners' doorway, *stage-left* who exits *stage-right*.) On one hand, de devil kips talking nonsense, and on de odder hand dere's Matilda.

(Sam is busy working and humming to himself and does not notice Lorna sneaking in behind him from *stage-right*. She is carrying a cloth bag of groceries and puts her hands over Sam's eyes.)

LORNA (In a disguised voice.) Guess who? (Mike sees Lorna and takes a newspaper and hides behind it. Sam prods gingerly at Lorna's rounded bag.)

SAM Don't tell me. Let me guess. Now dat feels round and soft lak somethin' nice. (Lorna giggles with each poke at her bag.) Now ... is it dat chubby chickadee in de Turners' house?

LORNA (She stops giggling.) What? Chubby what? Chickadee? What you mean, chubby chickadee? (Thinks.) You mean ... dat fat chicken in de Turners' kitchen. Well, lover boy. (She clobbers him with her grocery bag. He tries to explain, but she stomps her foot on his, and he hops about in agony.) Don't you cum near my doorstep, you hear! I'll strangle you! (Mike's newspaper shakes for a moment.)

SAM Lorna, baby. Hold on.

LORNA Don't you baby me, you two-timing Casanova. (Sam holds Lorna away from his feet as she stomps in anger.)

SAM Cool it, Lorna. Matilda don't mean nuttin' to me. (Mike's newspaper shakes visibly.)

LORNA (Coyly.) You mean dat? Hones' to goodness?

SAM Nuthing. You knows dat? And I knows dat?

LORNA And Matilda knows dat?

SAM Cross my heart and hope to die. (He crosses.)

LORNA (Happily.) You mean dat?

SAM What?

LORNA (Giggles.) Never mind what. I'm so happy I can jump ...

SAM You did already. Ow my big toe. (He groans.)

LORNA Oh, sorry hon. You ken cum over, I'll look at it.

SAM (Taking her grocery bag.) You're sure pretty when you get mad. Yore eyes lite up ...

LORNA I suppose chickadee's eyes are lightning bolts?

SAM   (Laughs.) Not lak yores, baby. Not lak yores. (Both exit, Sam hobbling and Lorna giggling as Sam leans on her shoulder, Masons' doorway *stage-right.*)

MIKE   Serves him right, getting clobbered. Two-timing Casanova. Hah! Next time, it might be a lethal weapon, then what? So I lost my imagination, eh? Well, I don't fancy getting wounded, maybe have a hospital bill I can't explain. (He continues to mutter to himself.)

(Enter Matilda from the Turners', *stage-left.* She is humming to herself, discoes a few steps uninhibitedly and laughs as she notices Mike talking to himself.)

MATILDA   Hiya Mike! You talking to yourself. You worrid or someting?

MIKE   Hi Matilda. Naw. I like to keep myself company. (They both laugh.)

MATILDA   Got any new funnies?

MIKE   Sure. You're my best customer. I always order the best. And the latest.

MATILDA   I've passed the hocus-pocus funnies on to Mrs. Turner. She likes the classics better. Easy reading wid de pictures in *Robinson Carusoo* ... *Tom Sawyer* ... and de killer white whale *Moby Dick.* Dat fish was sure mean. Worse dan *Jaws.* And *Jaws* was bad enough.

MIKE   Good! Now I can order more classic funnies for Mrs. Turner, and what's for you today? Wonder Woman? Superman? Outer space ...

MATILDA   Anything funny? Seems lak most of dem are shooting laser beams. How 'bout some hillbillies? I miss hearin' dem critters.

MIKE   (Laughs.) You lonesome for your hills in Kentucky?

MATILDA (Laughs.) Sometimes. But I don't get so lonesome, dat I wanna go back. I left dem hills for good for my in-laws. Dey can have 'em. And good riddance to my unsavory ex-husband. Dat good for nothing two-timing worm, ugh!

MIKE How about the Born Loser? Or Tarzan?

MATILDA Yeah! I like animals any time.

(Enters Sam *stage-right*. He sneaks behind Matilda and scares her.)

SAM Hiya Mama!

MATILDA (Jumps with fright.) Hey you. I ain't used to being hollered from behind. Come in front and talk lak a man.

SAM (Bussing her.) Hiya Mama!

MATILDA Well, if it ain't dat notoriety, Sam-m-muel Bull Grant! Lorna's always braggin' 'bout you. (Thinks.) Hey ... was you making a pass at me de first time you sed, Hiya Mama! or was you trying to read my funny book?

SAM (Laughs good naturedly.) Both! I heard you singin' dis morning. And I sed: Sam, dat Matilda has a voice lak a double bass. She ken sound lak syncopating jazz on one hand, den on de udder, lak a haunting coyote.

MATILDA (Laughing her head off.) Sam, you is kidding me lak a foxy coyote, but I love it. No wonder Lorna's head over heels in love wid you. My, you can talk nonsense, and make people feel good inside. Dat's wat I needed, hearing funny talk.

SAM And I sed ... Matilda's eyes muss lite up lak stars. Yeh! Magnetic! (Mike throws up his hands in despair.)

MATILDA Lak a come hither neon sign (Blinks with exaggeration.) wen I sings?

SAM Yeh! Real shine. (Both laugh and slap each other in fun.)

MATILDA Sam, I lak you. You got a genoowine sense of humor. (She pays Mike for her funny book.) If you're free tonight ...

SAM Yes, yes, yes?

MATILDA Cum over and see me. I'll mix you a free zombie. On de house.

SAM Hey mama, you mean dat? Wat 'bout de Turners?

MATILDA I'll tell 'em you helpin' me do dishes. Mrs. Turner approves me havin' extra help party times. See ya! (Exits Turners', *stage-left*.)

SAM See ya, Matilda! (Happily kicking a few karate chops with hands and legs.) How 'bout dat, Mike. Free zombies. I got invited to de stag party, de back door kind.

MIKE You know what?

SAM What, what, what?

MIKE You and Matilda ...

SAM Yeah, me and Matilda?

MIKE You and Matilda ... you two, you sure got a lot in common. Maybe that's the start of a meaningful relationship.

SAM Yeah? Wat's dat?

MIKE You both got a ... "genoowine" sense of humor. (They both laugh, like people sharing a joke. They resume their chores. Blackout.)

ACT I
Scene 2

The Scene:

The Turners' home looks like an Art Gallery with portraits of unsmiling people often found in courts of justice. One drawing is a backview of a nude female. *Downstage-right* is the front entrance and a bay window with a built-in bench. A palette shaped coffee table is in front of the window. *Upstage center* is a stairway leading to the upper floors. *Downstage-left* is the back entrance with a portable bar and two bar stools. The telephone is on the counter.

Stage Directions:

As the curtain rises, Matilda is preparing breakfast behind the counter and singing, humming to herself, adding secret ad libs mostly incoherent to anybody but herself. The phone rings.

MATILDA   Ring-a-ding-ding. Hello! Yes, dis is de Turners' residence. What? Oh, oh ... sure! Coming
up one Chadwick Turner. (She yells familiarly.)
CHAD-D-D, telephone. (Chad answers: Can't.)
Oh, oh. He can't come to de phone. He's sitting
on de throne, mebbe. (She guffaws at herself
then stops suddenly.) Oh, yes Miss Terry. Dat
is, I mean ... no, no, of course I wanna learn to
be couth, cóz uncouth is not nice, yes mam.
(Listens intently.) Yes Miss Terry. I'll start all
over again. Chad is INDISPOSED. Is dat better?
Good. Okay. I'll tell him when he's disposable.
(Hangs up.) Boy oh boy, what a pill. (Talks to
the phone.) I hates to work for you baby. Whew!
If Chad don't know any better to wear somethin'
decent, he ain't grown up. (Phone rings.) Ring-
a-ding-ding yourself. Hello! Who? Newspaper
reporter? Watta hell you want? Ain't been a
second gone wen somebuddy from de newspaper called. Oh, ain't you. Okay, okay ... so,
Chad, dat is, Mr. Chadwick Turner is indisposed.
But ̇dere's Mrs. Turner. Okay, I'll call her.
(Yells.) Mrs. Turner, Mrs. Turner! (*Offstage,*
Mrs. Turner answers: COMING! Enter stairway
upstage-center Mrs. Turner wearing a flapper
outfit of the twenties.)

MRS. TURNER: Hello! This is Mrs. Turner. (Listens then
giggles.) That's correct. My son is an Artist. He
loves to draw people in courtrooms ... you
know, richman, poorman, beggarman and lots
and lots of burglars. Someday ... he'll be as
famous as Daumier, he's French, you know.
Oh, you don't? I thought everybody knew
Daumier. Well of course he'll go to France, but
first, the itinerary, let me see, oh yes, first it's
Greece. He promised his father-in-law he'd

take Terry to see the Parthenon and take in a few Greek plays. (Laughs.) No, he doesn't understand a word of Greek, but he'll learn. He has time to learn. Then after Greece, it's ... Spain. Yes, of course, all of Picasso's country-men. What's that? (Laughs.) No he doesn't speak a word of Spanish. No ... he doesn't speak that either. He's an Artist. When he can't speak a language, he'll just draw a picture. (Giggles.) You're quite welcome. Goodbye! (Hangs up the phone.) Good morning, Matilda.

MATILDA Morning, Mrs. Turner. You look lak ... hm-m-m, well, it ain't *Gone wid de Wind*. Dey wore hoop skirts in dat pitcher.

MRS. TURNER Oh, I don't like anything literary. I just felt like ... oh, you know what I mean.

MATILDA Oh yes, Mrs. Turner, I know, but ... but ...

MRS. TURNER Oh, Matilda. Dress styles come and go, come and go. I always feel if I keep all my old clothes long enough, I'll have them to wear over and over.

MATILDA (Laughs.) Den you go ahead and wear any style you feel lak wearing, no matter if it's not roaring twenties styles yet.

MRS. TURNER Matilda ... you're a ... hm-m-m, a comfort, real comfort. Don't know what I would do without you.

MATILDA Dat's a comfort to know, for I dunno wat I'd do widout you and Chad. Mr. Turner, too, rest-in-peace, if he was here. And speaking of family, and a new one will make up ... I mean, join us ...

MRS. TURNER Oh, Terry. Chad loves her. She loves him.

MATILDA And we don't fit in dere family.

MRS. TURNER Well ... don't worry Matilda. We'll stick together anyway. We'll ... we'll manage to live happily ever after, too, with them.

MATILDA I hope Chad gets along wid Terry. Never mind bout de in-laws. Let Professor Mason go to Greece hisself. He shud have taken Terry dere hisself in de first place. Not expect Chad to do dat.

(Enter from *upstage stairway* Chad. He has a baggy tweed suit, leather elbow patches on his coat, turtleneck sweater. He looks debonaire with a bushy beard.)

CHAD Morning, ladies! What gossip have you been spreading? (Busses his mother. She protests his beard. Matilda laughs. Affectionate relationship of son-mother-Matilda is evident.)

MRS. TURNER Your public is clamoring to know about your wedding to be, your secret itinerary afterwards, et cetera.

MATILDA And we blabbed it all over to de newspapers. (They all laugh. The Turners sit at the counter and Matilda serves them breakfast.)

CHAD Well, I don't need any fanfare. I like being unnoticed. I learn more about people that way. They are unpretentious when they feel you are like them. Not some famous this or that. It would be terrible to be somebody. To find out that people like you not for your talent, whatever it may be, but for being famous, a somebody.

MATILDA You tell 'em, boy. Dat's my Chad.

CHAD Knowing you Matilda and mother, knowing your love ... feeling it, that's what counts. (Mrs. Turner kisses her son.)

MATILDA Oh, before I forgit ... Terry called wid her kisses blown in de telephone, jes' for you, 'cept you wasn't at de odder end listening.

CHAD Oh, she wants me to call her?

MATILDA No. She wants you to ... to ... not to forget your luncheon at de country club.

CHAD Oh my, I forgot. Can't. You tell her I have to be in court again, another murder. Got to get sketches in for TV. This evening news.

MATILDA I don't wanna talk to her ... dat is, mebbe you better get used to talking to yore future wife, and ... dat way, wen you have to break a date de lass minute ... you knows how to talk excuses.

CHAD Then ... I have to stop by to invite a few friends who didn't get a written invitation. Some people insist on written invitations before going to a party. Can't come unless they see it in writing. Anyway, a personal invitation, straight from the horse's mouth ...

MATILDA You wanna know somethin'?

CHAD What?

MATILDA Oh never mind.

MRS. TURNER Oh go ahead Matilda. Spit it out.

MATILDA Terry will be mad you stood her up for lunch, but ... I know de bride is not welcum at her husband's stag party, but ... I ain't goin' tell her 'bout dat, only 'bout the lunch. Busy and crimminal courts, et cetera. No party stuff, and *indisposed.*

CHAD Thanks Matilda, you're a pal.

MRS. TURNER Seems a pity there'll be men, only, at your stag tonight. But then, a stag is a stag, isn't it?

CHAD Well, as a matter of fact, there'll be couple females, too, nice models, Lena and Rita.

MATILDA Oh ho. Now he tells us. How will Terry like dat?

CHAD That's Lena's rearend, the redhead, over there. I just wanted a few people over for a drink, those who are not invited to the wedding. After all, you know how it is ... the Masons' house is too small ...

MATILDA Sure. Not gonna tell Terry nuthin'. (Laughs.)

90

CHAD And then, there's you ... and Matilda. Proper chaperones.

MRS. TURNER Well ... I'm glad I have a horse invitation. I usually like the written kind, myself, but I accept graciously, thank you son.

CHAD And you can serve weak cocktails as usual, so nobody gets drunk.

MATILDA Shirley Temples coming up, long drinks, fancy long drinks, mebbe with swivel sticks wid olives or cherries and lots and lots of crackers/cheeses/tiny orrdervesses.

CHAD And if you and mother get bored with my friends, you can both go to bed.

MATILDA Me, get tired? No way.

MRS. TURNER Really, Matilda. You heard what Chad said. We might get tired and bored chit-chatting. That's a good idea (Thinks.) to go to bed when one tires.

MATILDA Ain't nuttin' wrong wid fighting fatigue, but, if I have to, I'll get tired chit-chatting. (Doorbell chimes. Enter Professor Mason in a dignified business suit.) Coming! Oh, Good morning Professor.

MASON Good Morning Katherine, Chad, Matilda. Now that it is a matter of hours before we belong to one family, I let myself in, the door was unlocked. (Chad and Mrs. Turner laugh and exchange handshakes. Matilda returns to her counter.) My, you look ... as if you're reading the *Great Gatsby*? How charming ...

MRS. TURNER Wrong again Henry. I'm reading "How to dance the Charleston." It's marvelous therapy for my arthritis. See ... (Demonstrates slowly kicking up right heel to hit her behind, then left heel, ending with a slow motion hands on knees and opening them outward with uninhibited groans of pain.) It's wonderful therapy. You should try it, Henry. (Chad and Matilda laugh.)

MASON I don't have arthritis. (Amused but serious.) Of course, I'll have to give it a try sometime. Whatever you teach yourself, that's marvelous. I wish my students had initiative like you. No initiative to read to learn. I got 'em reading "Desire Under the Elms." The title ... well. Seems like TV ads work. The title got to 'em. They liked the play, once they read it. Now I've got 'em reading Eugene O'Neill's "Hairy Ape." Most of them thought it was a TV series. Part of "The Planet of the Apes."

CHAD I've got to go, Dad. Any message for me? Terry okay?

MASON Oh, of course, message. (Reads notebook.) Tell my gloriously bearded Samson I'll see him at lunch, and is there a stag tonight? Lorna says, Sam says, there is. Well, is there?

MRS. TURNER Chad has invited a few friends for a cocktail, men only.

MATILDA And two nice models, Lena and Rita.

CHAD And mother and Matilda, that makes four females.

MASON Splendid. I'll tell Terry. Now I must be on my way. (Turns to leave with Chad, then hesitates.) Bye son, I'll have to talk to your mother for a second. (Exit Chad *stage-right.*)

MATILDA Coffee, Professor Mason?

MASON Thank you Matilda. Please. Black. No sugar, no cream.

MRS. TURNER Over here, Matilda, on the coffee table. (They sit at bay window.)

MASON I don't know how to begin.

MRS. TURNER Well we can start with the weather. Everybody does that.

MASON Well ... (Amused.) Terry and I have been talking ...

MRS. TURNER Oh dear. Is something wrong?

MASON No, no, see, I don't know how to begin.

MATILDA Mebbe a chugalug of my coffee ken help break da ice. My coffee is so strong ... et cetera. (Mason and Mrs. Turner laugh with Matilda.)

MASON Terry ... Well, she is a bit domineering, and she thinks it would be best if Lorna came over here. You see ... Lorna, well, Terry and Lorna ... Oh, Terry told me another thing. Tell me truthfully, Katherine. Did you tell Terry you were moving?

MRS. TURNER (Confused.) Moving? Well ... well, of course I thought about it. I didn't say when I'd move, but of course, I, I ... I did think about moving, sometime. And if Terry wants Lorna to come here, of course Matilda and I can ...

MATILDA (Bluntly.) Well I ken carry Mrs. Turner's stuff to yore house, to Terry's room. Ain't nobody gonna be dere. And I may as well move over dere myself in Lorna's room.

MRS. TURNER (Embarrassed.) Oh, Matilda, really. I, I wouldn't think of doing such a thing ... this is so embarrassing, I mean ... I couldn't ... I hadn't thought about anything lately, Henry.

MASON (Laughs.) Well I must say, this is amusing. Almost like a Victorian comedy.

MATILDA Only Terry means it for real. She is mistress of dis house. And being in-laws, I don't mind telling her who is and who ain't mistress. (Mason and Mrs. Turner laugh.)

MASON I always said Matilda has a pragmatic approach to life. If the circumstances weren't a bit awkward. Well, as a matter of fact, I thought I'd paint Terry's room and ...

MRS. TURNER Oh, I've read a how-to book: "Paint your attic, your spare room. Tackle it yourself." It's an Interior Decorating book. (Breathlessly.) You must let me help you, Henry.

MATILDA And me too. If I havta live in an attic, I may as well paint it, too.

MASON (Amused.) Yes, yes, of course. (Thinks.) You know ... I'm glad I'm inheriting in-laws with a keen, Victorian sense of humor. Don't get up. I'll see myself out. Bye, ladies. (Exits chuckling, *stage-right.*)

MRS. TURNER Bye Henry. Have a nice day. (She looks out the bay window and sighs.)

MATILDA He sure is good lookin' for his age. Ain't he, Mrs. Turner?

MRS. TURNER What?

MATILDA Professor Mason. He sure is good lookin', not too old, neither. Mebbe he could stand a toupee right on the top, den he could get by for being forty.

MRS. TURNER (Laughs.) Yes, he is pleasant and charming. He's polite too. He always compliments me in whatever I am reading.

MATILDA Mebbe, it make sense ...

MRS. TURNER What makes sense?

MATILDA Well, ain't none of my business, but ... if, just if sometime a male looks good to a female, like sometimes birds have funny habits, like the bees, too ...

MRS. TURNER Matilda, will you come to the point?

MATILDA Well you said it, not me. The point is ... If Professor Mason looks nice and acts nice to you, he'd make a good ketch. So ... (Emphatically.) Why don't you ketch 'im while the ketching's good.

MRS. TURNER (Horrified.) Goodness gracious, Matilda. (She shakes her head, goes *upstage-center.*) If I didn't know you so well, I'd say those comic books you read give you funny ideas. Why ... how could you? He's a professor of ... (Gets upset at not being able to think of anything to say, throws up hands exasperatedly and exits *stairway.*)

MATILDA Sorry, Mrs. Turner. (Giggles then resumes chores, ad libs while singing, Moskeeters am a hummin' on de honeysuckle vine ... yeah you pesky moskeeters ... sweet Kentucky babe ... hums as the curtain comes down.)

ACT I
Scene 3

The Scene:

It is evening. The counter is lit with a candelabrum. Finger food is on the counter and on the coffee table. Matilda is working behind the bar shining glasses.

(Enter Lorna, *stage-left*. She cranes her neck into the room. Matilda spots her.)

MATILDA Well, well. Is yo' a bloodhound or beagle?

LORNA (Belligerently.) Miss Terry's outside. Don't you talk to me lak dat again, in dat voice, or I'll tell Sam come black yore eyes. (Exits snorting, as Terry enters.)

MATILDA (Laughs.) Won't give Sam no zombies, if he dares. (Sees Terry.) Good evening, Miss Terry.

TERRY I'm so excited Matilda. Good evening. I thought I'd come early just to peek. (She fusses at the counter, tastes and approves. Goes to the coffee table, then looks out the bay window.)

MATILDA Don't see no reason why you don't stay. You can leave, like Mrs. Turner and me, when we get tired chitchatting. Dere's two other females.

TERRY Yes, I know. Dad told me. Lena and Rita. What do they do?

MATILDA Yeah. Models. (Starts to point at the nude painting of Lena, then hesitates, pretends to squash a mosquito.) Darn insect, you.

TERRY   What kind of party will this be? Proper, I hope. Nothing scandalous?

MATILDA Cocktails, Miss Terry. I makes the ordervesses and drinks.

TERRY   (Smiles.) Those models ... they'll keep their clothes on, won't they?

MATILDA I hopes so. If dey don't, I say ... (Thinks.) naughty, naughty.

TERRY   (Giggles.) No. Don't do that Matilda. So what if models want to take off their clothes and let Artists sketch them. I think Chad will be famous as an Artist. Another Daumier. Do you know Daumier?

MATILDA No, Miss Terry, except something 'bout Daumier drawing washer wimmen, and poor people in France, third-rate class people.

TERRY   (Giggles.) That's about it. So Chad has a chance with his drawing court scenes and criminals, and all those people who seem to kill one another. He'll be famous one day. Rich and famous.

MATILDA I never been in a courthouse before, but by de looks of dese pictures, nobody is happy dere. I like the Zoo better ... birds, apes ...

TERRY   (Laughs.) You are a card, Matilda.

MATILDA Well ... I hope a high trump. (Laughs.) Doorbell chimes.) Don't worry, Miss Terry. I'll take good care of the next Daumier. (Terry exits hurriedly *stage-left* as Matilda answers the door, *stage-right. Offstage* Chad yells, I'll be right down.) Good evening Lena and Rita! My, Chad was right. You are glamorous, you two. Real pretty.

LENA   Well, Matilda, Chad has spoken of you so much, nice to meetcha.

RITA   What a lovely gallery. Good evening, Matilda. Where's Chad?

MATILDA He is indisposed, but he'll be right down.

(Enter Chad from center stairway.)

CHAD   Hey, hey, ladies. Glad you could come. (He busses Lena and admires Rita's dress.) Dance, pretty lady? Matilda, a slow something, soft music ... (Latin American music is played.)

RITA   You have a lovely gallery. Perfectly loverly ...

CHAD   Thank you. Don't talk, dance. Let me hold you, h-m-m, smell sweet, too.

RITA   Don't talk. Dance. This is your last chance to dance with other women.

CHAD   Oh now, don't sound sad. I'll dance with you any day.

RITA   No you won't. Not after tonight.

CHAD   Well, give me a reason why I shouldn't.

RITA   Don't talk. Just dance. Close your eyes and dream ...

CHAD   Okay, okay, I like holding you close and dancing. Favorite pastimes. (Terry has tiptoed into the room and is horrified at seeing Chad with eyes closed dancing with Rita. She stomps out and slams door.) What was that?

MATILDA   Must be an angry wind on de back doah. It's shut now. (Doorbell rings.)

CHAD   I'll get it. (Enter Professor Mason, who is embarrassed about something.) Dad, surprise, surprise. Come on in. Have a drink. This is Rita. and that (Points.) is Lena. (Girls exchange Hi!) Professor Mason!

MASON   Terry ... I missed Terry and Lorna said ... I didn't know what it was, Lorna ran out of the house. I thought ... well, if Terry, well if Terry's not here ...

LENA   Hi again, professor Mason. Will I do?

CHAD   Oh Dad, come on in and dance with Lena. (He dances away with Rita.)

MASON   Well I must be going.

LENA (In a babyish voice.) Will you tell mama why? Can mama come, too?

MASON Goodness ... I don't mean to be rude, but I don't dance.

LENA (Laughs out loud.) Why didn't you say so. My fifth husband didn't dance either.

MASON Your fifth husband. Goodness. You look very young to have had five husbands.

LENA Well to tell the truth, it was only three husbands. I didn't want to tie myself down legally, so I just moved in and moved out with husband four and five. I'm liberated. A modern liberal.

MASON How extraordinary! Like a character right out of Boccaccio.

LENA Who is he?

MASON Who?

LENA Boccaccio? An Artist?

MASON No, a writer, yes ... he was an artist in the creative sense. What I mean ... you see, there I go again. I have no way of knowing how to begin a social conversation ... really I must be going. I can't dance, no good at talking ... I guess I am strictly a ... traditional professor, dull and dimwitted ...

LENA Now don't you worry. Nobody ever was unhappy with my dancing. I used to work the dance halls for 10 cents a dance.

MASON You don't say? That was a bargain.

LENA Now, I won't charge. It's free. (Lena starts dancing in front of him saying, cha, cha, cha.)

MASON Oh, you don't understand. I just teach ... teach American Drama. (Lena stops short.)

LENA So? Don't tell me there's no dancing in American drama?

MASON (Laughs embarrassingly.) No. I don't mean no dancing in American drama. Look at O'Neill. Well, there's not dancing in his plays like the musical *Oklahoma.* Drama, after all, is dialogue. More dialogue than dance.

LENA Sh-h-h, don't say another word. Mama knows. Relax and say cha-cha-cha like me. Or, just count out loud, ONE and a TWO.

MASON (Apprehensively.) I'm afraid my sense of rhythm ... it's not tuned up. What I mean is, my joints are a bit stiff from not using them. (Lena had not made any headway in front of him. She slips behind him and puts her hands on his waist. He is ticklish and protests with giggles.) Oh, dear-r-r Lena? I can-n-not dance. He-e-e-e! I can't kick up my heels.

LENA (In a baby voice.) Never mind, baby. Just say ONE, and a TWO, and I'll say cha-cha-cha. ONE and a TWO, and a STEP and a STEP with a LEFT and a RIGHT. (Mason has assumed a diagonal awkward waddling stance saying ONE and a TWO, hitting his legs for a LEFT and a RIGHT with Lena pushing him and encouraging him with giggling cha-cha-chas. They concentrate on their feet, circle the stage ending *upstage center*; enter Mrs. Turner, who applauds with the rest. Mrs. Turner is elegantly attired in an evening dress of the 20's.)

MRS. TURNER Oh Henry! You were wonderful. I must let you borrow my book on the Charleston.

MASON (Flustered.) Madam, good evening. (He takes her aside *downstage-right*.) I never will ... I never was ... I. What can I say? This is ridiculous.

MRS. TURNER That was quite a caper. I didn't know you were coming to the party.

MASON Katherine, how shall I begin? I've never done anything so humiliating, dancing, I don't know what step it was only ONE and a TWO.

MRS. TURNER I say ONE TWO when I dance, then I KICK, KICK, KICK, KICK. It's in the body movement, one has to feel the rhythm.

MASON Well ... I've had enough body movement for one evening. I was looking for Terry when this happened. I had no intentions of coming ... of dancing. I don't fancy cavorting ... (Doorbell chimes.)

CHAD I'll get it. (He goes to *stage-right* and opens door to antlered artist friends in leotards and far-out costumes who mime fantasy greetings before collapsing *stage-left* to applaud others following. As soon as the last mime is finished, Mason and Mrs. Turner move aside. The guests mingle.)

MASON Well, I don't know how ... what to do? What I am expected to do at this time and place? Should I, or shouldn't I look for Terry ... or stay at this fabulous, enchanting, far-out party. (He nods appreciatively.)

MRS. TURNER Oh Henry! You must stay and dance with me.

MASON (Aghast.) Madam ...

MRS. TURNER I don't know how to dance the Charleston, but you can do your cha-cha bit, and ... I'll follow.

MASON (Laughing uncomfortably.) You know Katherine, at my age. At our age ... now, how is it, that I can't begin a perfectly good line of social chitchat. I can memorize the lines in a play, those powerful words written by imaginative playwrights ... I am perfectly comfortable with reading idiot boards for television ... yet ... why is it, I can't, simply can't chitchat? Do you know what I mean?

MRS. TURNER You know Henry ... that is my problem, too. Maybe in a way, we are not the chitchatting type of people.

MASON (Smiles.) I'm glad we can see something eye to eye.

MRS. TURNER And if we can do what these young people are doing cheek to cheek, maybe we won't stand out like some sore thumbs.

MASON (Chuckles.) Well ... it seems like the young ones are ignoring us anyway, so let me recapitulate.

MRS. TURNER What's that? Recapitulate?

MASON Oh, that's a way I have of thinking how to perform ... a catch your breath ...

MRS. TURNER Is it difficult to perform without recapitulating, et cetera ...?

MASON Sh-h-h-h don't say a word. Okay, madam, may I have this dance?

MRS. TURNER Delighted! (They take up a tango open position, cheek to cheek, and dance slowly in that crunched position, obviously delighted with their seemingly awkward but final attempt at dancing, cross *downstage-left*. Doorbell chimes. Silence. Loud rapping at the door.)

CHAD Who can that be? I'll get it ...(Crosses *downstage-right* to front door. A sultan and masculine Scheherazade enter ..)

SULTAN You are my subject, Chadwick Turner?

CHAD Yes, well, I live here, I'm Chadwick Turner. Who are you?

SULTAN Who do you think? In my multi-million dollar costume of my country?

CHAD A sultan, I can see that. (Everyone is whispering and laughing.)

SULTAN I am the great, great, great son of a gun, from the great, great, great desert of ... outside of what's it, you know my country, I presume?

SCHEHERAZADE (Coyly in a high pitched voice waving her scarf at Chad.) And I am Scheherazade from another country, but I live in his country. And I tell him stories, so he won't ... kill me. Oh ... I live in fear.

CHAD (Shouting.) Taco and Bill ... Crazy, man. (Everyone claps, whistles, laughs, chants, "dance, Scheherazade ... Dance." Feet stomp, loud whistles, claps, quiet.)

SCHEHERAZADE In this day and age of disco dancing, I feel ... I feel ... akin, yet ...

SULTAN Woman from my harem, hold thy prattling tongue. Amuse us with a mime. Or off with your head! (Claps, feet stomping and whistles, then music. Middle East belly dancing rhythm and a mime of some sort with spotlight on sultan and Scheherazade. End with shouts of "encore, encore," whistling, feet stomping. Then a loud knocking at the front door. Quiet, and doorbell chimes.)

CHAD Now who could that be? (Opens front door; enter two police officers *downstage-left*.) Officers ... Good evening! Can I do anything? Is something wrong?

POLICEWOMAN Who is Chadwick Turner?

CHAD I am. Is something wrong?

POLICEMAN The lady across the street says you are disturbing the peace.

CHAD What lady across the ...? The one directly across? Or the one further up ...?

POLICEWOMAN A Ms. Mason asked that we investigate. Can't sleep with the ruckus.

POLICEMAN Hey, what kind of a party is going on. It's not Halloween yet? Or is it? Hey, I get it. Play acting and stuff.

POLICEWOMAN We just heard a little bit of hooting and shouting and whistling, but if this has been going on so it disturbs people, well ...

MASON I say officers, perhaps, we can be a little less noisy, then, maybe, do you suppose ... we could have a nightcap and leave quietly?

POLICEMAN Excellent idea. That is the best chitchat I've heard all evening. Wish we could join ya, but we're on duty. So ...

POLICEWOMAN One for the road, and keep the noise down. Night! (Exit officers *downstage-right*. There is a scurry for last minute drinks and finger food, then some will exit *downstage-left*, thanking Chad before leaving. Chad slips out *downstage-left*, too. Mason and Mrs. Turner say goodnight to the rest exiting *downstage-right*. Matilda is cleaning up the room humming to herself. Guests are gone.)

MASON I won't say this to Chad, but my headstrong, outspoken, young ... sweet child Terry was sure mad about something to call the police.

MRS. TURNER Oh dear! And right before the wedding! Is this supposed to be auspicious ... like fortune telling or star gazing, one must take the good with the bad?

MASON Are you asking a question or just ... just ...

MRS. TURNER Oh dear! You don't suppose Terry wants to leave Chad at the altar? Chad jilted?

MASON Hardly. Although, I'm not sure. What a night! Such talent! Costumes.

MRS. TURNER I think I like dancing, too. (Both laugh.)

MASON We didn't do so badly, despite our ... in spite of ...

MRS. TURNER Yes. Matilda, some brandy, please.

MATILDA One brandy coming up. (Mason and Mrs. Turner sit *downstage-right*, window seats and Matilda takes two snifters and a bottle to the palette shaped coffee table. She returns to the kitchen counter, takes two glasses, a bottle, exits *downstage-left* humming to herself.)

MASON Well, this has been an exciting night. Something I would never have encountered in my own house. All those people under one roof. An artist's roof.

MRS. TURNER Wonderful, wonderful party, even if it was a short-short party. I do hope, nothing happens ... what I mean Terry is not unhappy ...

MASON (Sipping his brandy and liking it.) Terry will be ... Well, Terry has always had her way. Since she was nine. Her mother ... left us so suddenly ...

MRS. TURNER Oh I'm so sorry.

MASON That was ten years ago.

MRS. TURNER Oh ... Terry must have missed her mother.

MASON On the contrary. Terry and I ... well her mother was a bridge fiend.

MRS. TURNER Bridge?

MASON Yes, playing bridge. I like playing bridge, but not like Terry's mother. It was one marathon after another. Got to be that I just dropped out. Couldn't stand the pressure, and for what? Nothing ... well, that is what I ... anyway, Terry and I didn't mind staying at home reading to each other. And Terry would tell Lorna what to cook for our supper. At first, it was like Terry was playing an adult role, ordering Lorna to use a French Cookbook, or a Danish Pastry Cookbook ... I thought it was wonderful at first. Then when her mother passed away, Terry ordered Lorna, and me, too. She and Lorna shopped for everything, groceries, my clothes, Lorna's, hers. She kept up with styles ...

MRS. TURNER And now, nineteen ... Terry will have her own life in this house. Do you suppose she likes these paintings?

MASON (Laughs.) I don't know. That is one thing about marriage. One matures. And I hope they come to some agreement on what stays on the walls. Oh, my goodness.

MRS. TURNER What is it?

MASON What happened to Chad? It's getting late. I forgot about Terry.

MRS. TURNER He probably went over to the lady across the street. Here, have another whiff of brandy.

MASON Thank you. I should be getting home. The wedding is tomorrow morning. (He looks at his watch.) I'll give those young pups exactly ten minutes to growl. Then out, out! (He looks around.) Where's Matilda?

MRS. TURNER She probably went out for comic books. Strange, we've lived in this neighborhood for the last ten years, watched people move in, move out, even noticed the first high rise condominium against our backyards ... all the new faces to live with, yet I never knew ... I didn't meet you, until Terry and my son ... suddenly, we're in-laws.

MASON That's city life. Everybody is afraid of his neighbor. It was worse in New York City. Manhattan. Tonight ... all those strange faces and costumes took me back 30 years, near Columbia. The International House. Isn't that a coincidence? It was the first time then, that I lived under the same roof with strange, exotic people ... it was a wonderful time of my life, so I like to remember New York that way, we lived in such a sheltered dormitory ... then afterwards, when we were married, had an apartment ... goodness, we couldn't trust anybody. Doors always broken in, windows smashed, so different. Funny how one is resilient ... adjusts to anything when one is young. We loved the plays, ballets, operas, museums and ... bought new locks all the time. (Both laugh.)

MRS. TURNER San Francisco has always had plays, ballets, operas, museums too, though not as many as New York. We've always lived here, in this house it seems, that is, until my husband ... late husband inherited a fortune. Then we went here and there on cruises, cocktail parties here, there, everywhere, an alcoholic stump, you might say. Poor Richard, he loved brandy, like Winston Churchill, couldn't give it up until the last. We had enough money for the best ills, but ... whoosh ... money can't buy everything.

MASON Chad mentioned that ... his father was a wonderful psychologist, loved to experiment with rats in mazes, cats, dogs, monkeys, pigeons.

MRS. TURNER Yes, he was marvelous with those animals. Then Aunt Phina died. It· was his mother's sister. Married an oilman. Strange how money changes people. He forgot his animals ... even quit analyzing me. Told me I was a riddle. He enjoyed brandy, too much of it.

MASON If somebody gave me a pot of gold, I'd enjoy brandy, too. I really must be getting home Katherine. (Rises.) Now I must see myself to the door. Don't get up. Goodnight! (Exits *stage-right*. Mrs. Turner says "Good Night, Henry," then sits for a moment before turning to look out the window. She gets up slowly, stares at the floor for a moment to remember something, puts her hands on her hips and dances awkwardly saying cha-cha-cha, ONE TWO. Exits *upstage stairway*.)

(Enter Matilda and Sam, *Downstage-left.*)

MATILDA Come in, Sam. Help me wid de dishes.

SAM Okay, honey bun.

MATILDA Yo can sit at de counter, for a starter.

SAM (Sits.) Tanks, Matilda. Dem zombies was terrific. Let's make one for de road. An eye opener. My, my, (Blinks at all the paintings.)

MATILDA One weak zombie coming up!

SAM Chad do all des criminals?

MATILDA Yeah. He's got talent. All free hand. No camera snapping. First hand down at de criminal court.

SAM Hi dere, Tom. Hey dat's Tom. He's my friend. Wat he doing in criminal court? He couldn't hurt nuthin'.

MATILDA Now, let's see. Dat dere Tom got on de stand as a witness. Chad draws criminals and witness, all dem in the court, even judges, and jury people. He keeps busy drawing 'em all. Don't know all de history of dese people, but Chad knows. Chad is like Daumier.

SAM Yeah. Do I know Daumier?

MATILDA No, Daumier is French. Don't know why Daumier would draw criminals and third-class peoples in France, especially wen the can-can girls are prettier in the Follies Beejare, but you know artists. All kinds of peoples interest dem. And some day, Chad will be famous lak Daumier.

SAM Yo don't say. And I'll say, hey, I know Chad. He's my friend. Lak Tom. Tom will be famous, too. Hey, ain't dat somethin'.

MATILDA (Gives him a drink.) Here's to happiness of Chad and Terry.

SAM I'll drink to dat again. (Drinks.) You know, Matilda, wid each zombie, you looks like a rare orchid.

MATILDA (Laughs.) Sh-h-h-h not so loud. If you wasn't
     dat wildcat Lorna's property, I'd mix 'nough
     zombies so you sees me ... lak an ord'nary rose.
     (Both laugh then sh-h-h each other.)

SAM   I'm starved.

MATILDA Eat up. I made all dem ordervesses.

SAM   Yeah? (Sam eats several finger foods, then
     hesitates and thinks.) Delicious. Only ... why?
     How come?

MATILDA Why what ...? Speak up, man!

SAM   Why don't you make jumbo sardine sand-
     wiches? (Matilda laughs, sh-h-hs him, they
     both giggle as they enjoy their repast.)

CURTAINS.

ACT II
Scene I

The Scene: Same as ACT I, Scene I, Kiosk, people, early morning, except Sam is now wearing a suit as he goes about humming, shining shoes, brushing people. Then there is a lull.

SAM   Gotta leave soon. Important date.

MIKE   Yeah? Must be real important. What's so ... important that you're wearing a suit? You wear suits more often these days.

SAM   Lorna likes me to wear a suit. Sez, it's ... like people in a real store, the owners, I mean. I kent explain it. I kent even spell de word. It's French ... (Pronounces exactly.) entrepreneur.

MIKE   You don't say. Hey, that's great ... entrepreneur. She wants you to wear a suit like an entrepreneur?

SAM   No, not her.

MIKE   Not her? Well, if you're not wearing a suit for her, who ... wants you to ... well, it's none of my business, but you sure been talking nonsense these last few days.

SAM   (Laughs.) Well, you see ... Lorna sez, dat ...

MIKE   Serious, eh, you and Lorna?

SAM   Oh hell! You'd laugh at me, anyway.

MIKE   Laugh? Why laugh? Am I a laughing person? I can't figure you out, Sam. All of a sudden, you start wearing suits. As if you're trying to impress somebody. And it ain't Lorna.

SAM	(Laughs again.) Well, it's Lorna's brother ...
MIKE	Lorna's brother?
SAM	Yeah.
MIKE	You want to impress him?
SAM	No, I don't want to impress him. Yes, and No. You know what I mean?
MIKE	Well, I'm trying to figure out what you mean, but it's okay, never mind. How you feeling today? Okay?
SAM	Ain't been feeling well, neither. Getting kinda mixed up.
MIKE	You going to the doctor? You should, if you don't feel good. Precautionary.
SAM	Naw, I'm okay. Don't need a doc. Maybe it's my teeth.
MIKE	(Concerned.) Cavity? You got some cavities?
SAM	Naw. Wisdom tooth. Yeah, dat's it. If Lorna's brother come by, tell him I ain't here, coz I took time out to go to de dentist. Yeah. Dat odder do it. All entrepreneurs are de own bosses, and ... (Laughs.) I shouldda taught of dat.
MIKE	You have a wisdom tooth ... that you have to fill?
SAM	Well, if ... if he asks about my wisdom tooth, tell him I gotta pull it, and I got insurance to pull it and pay for it. Yeah. Got it?
MIKE	(Thinks.) H-m-m-m. Don't know yet, but eventually I'll figure it out. (Enter Lorna from the Turners' doorway, *stage-left*. She is dressed in a lovely short, bridal costume.)
LORNA	(Excitedly.) Hiya Mike! Here I is, honey bun! How do I look?
SAM	Hey .. .smashing!

MIKE	Hi Lorna! Yeah, you look snazzy. You gonna go with Sam to the dentist?
SAM	Hey Mike, in case I don't come back, will you close up?
MIKE	Sure Sam. Don't I always? (Thinks.)
LORNA	What dentist?
SAM	Oh never mind. Let's go. (Lorna and he start to leave, *downstage-right,* but Lorna stops.)
LORNA	You got a toothache Sam?
MIKE	Wisdom tooth. Maybe it has to come out.
LORNA	(Giggling suddenly.) Oh you kidding Mike. (Laughs.) Wisdom tooth? Sam already has falsies. (Exit *downstage-right.*)
MIKE	Oh. H-m-m-m. What was that all about? Maybe I'm getting old. (Grins.) Well, I ain't that old, not to notice a few things happening. That foxy Sam. At last Lorna has you round her finger, hah! (Chuckles, busies himself. Enter Mason, *doorway* to his house, *downstage-right.* He looks as if he had slept in his suit all night.)
MIKE	Morning, Professor Mason! Nice morning.
MASON	Morning. (He thumbs through some comic books slowly.)
MIKE	I saw Lorna leaving. She looks well.
MASON	I'm glad she's taking care of Chad's house, moving all Terry's things over. I kinda miss ... Matilda is fine, only I got used to Lorna ...
MIKE	Chad and Terry should be bicycling over the Basque Mountains by now.
MASON	(Perks up.) Yeah! Over the ... mountains, Basque mountains ... How did you know that?
MIKE	Lorna told me.
MASON	Lorna told you?
MIKE	Well she told Sam.
MASON	Lorna told Sam?
MIKE	Yeah, going backwards, I got the news from Sam, who got the news from Lorna, who heard it from Matilda, who said you got a letter from Chad and Terry.

MASON Does this grapevine work all the time? Backwards and forward?

MIKE Yeah! We've been enjoying Europe second-hand.

MASON Amazing. (Thinks.) Do you hear all your news that way?

MIKE About Chad and Terry?

MASON About everything ... whatever happens in our house?

MIKE Well, most everything, especially about Europe ... we sort of pump Matilda for news. The Parthenon ... the open amphitheatres in Greece ... El Greco's Toldeo ... Picasso's Guernica ... Goya ...

MASON (Brightly.) Katherine and I must take a trip someday ... to see the Greeks, the famous plays in the natural setting, the amphitheatres. I think Katherine would like that.

MIKE How's Mrs. Turner-Mason? She's okay? Matilda says ...

MASON (Remembers.) Oh, Mrs. Turner-Mason is fine. Now, let's see, comic books? No. Oh yes. A *Vogue,* please.

MIKE She looked tired. She must be working hard. Matilda says ...

MASON Yes. She is lonesome, missed the kids. So she went home. To her house. (Assertive suddenly.) Maybe this comic book, yes ... yes, yes, *Monitor, Vogue* and comic book. Matilda can share our literature, too. (He pays Mike who looks after him exiting Turners' doorway, *downstage-left.* Mike laughs to himself, busies himself. Blackout.)

ACT II
Scene 2

The Scene:

The Masons' house is the reverse of the Turners'. The back entrance and kitchenette is *downstage-right* with an added dining table and four chairs with ruffled cushions. *Upstage-center* is the same stairway to the second floor. *Downstage-left* is the front entrance with a rocking chair in front of the bay window with the built-in bench. Except for one print of Winslow Homer's painting, the wall spaces have books and accents of pioneering days in the United States.

Stage Directions:

Matilda is fussing with the place settings at the table, trying to remember where the spoons and forks should be and rearranging them carefully. The phone rings.

MATILDA Ring-a-ding-ding! (She exaggerates a pose, clears her throat, and formally announces with perfect diction the following words.) Th-th-th-th-th-this is th-th-the Masons' residence. (Laughs suddenly.) Dat you Lorna? Well, well, well. How's de luvbirds? Congratulations and ... (Seriously.) Don't cry Lorna. I can't unnderstand you. Yeah. You don't say. He do dat? You do dat? No kidding. All becoz ... Oh my! Well honey, dat ain't bad, one in-law. Tell him to get used to it. You did? Sure, sure. Don't you worry none, Lorna. Sam loves you, and you still love him, don't you? Sure. But don't do nuthin' rash. Yes, Yes, I'll tell 'em you'll stay wid 'em. I hope dey had a nice trip ... and dey is happier than you and Sam, and de old folks, too. Yeah. Don't worry Lorna. Jest kip trying. (Hangs up and laughs.) One month, and Sam's marriage is on de rocks. Hah! All becoz a brudder-in-law moves in. (Chuckles.) Don't blame Sam. I never got used to mine. Cum to think of it, I couldn't stand my husband, dat two-timing rat. (The doorbell rings.) Chad? Terry? Oh ... Mrs. Turner-Mason, Professor Mason! Dey's here. Th-th-they are here! (Enter *downstage-left* a belligerent Terry and a beaten Chad.) Welcome home, Terry ... Chad.
TERRY Hello Matilda! Awk! Oh! What happened to the furniture, my modern ... where's my stereo, and my spider plants?
CHAD Hello Matilda. (They hug each other.) Good to see ya! Where's mòm? And dad?
MATILDA Upstairs arguing. (Chad laughs.)
TERRY (Angrily.) It's ... it's ... I don't like ruffles. So colonial. This is the twentieth century.

MATILDA Mrs. Turner-Mason likes ruffles. And ... Professor Mason, he is getting to like ruffles.

TERRY (Nastily.) It's ugly. (She stomps around. Enter Mrs. Turner-Mason *stairway center-stage* followed by Mason. They are both wearing colonial costumes, wigs and all. Mrs. TM starts sniffling and runs to Chad. Terry has started to bawl and Mason goes to her.)

MRS. TURNER-MASON: I'm so happy, that I'm crying with joy.

MATILDA If everybody sits and eats and talks, breakfast is coming up. (All comply.)

MASON Good idea. Did you have a good trip?

TERRY Long and boring. Like sitting in a strait jacket. Nowhere to go. Just sit.

CHAD Non-stop, Zurich, New York, San Francisco. Fast jets. Still tiring. We had movies. Papillon. Wonderful acting. Didn't you like the acting? Dustin ...

TERRY Criminals on Devil's Island. Rather primitive penal code.

CHAD Didn't you like the acting? At least we understood what they were saying. It was not like the plays in the amphitheatre. Hard rocks to sit on. Wind blowing. Impressive, yes, but I can't remember anything except the title, and the actress moaning Orestes ... Orestes and those other Greek plays.

TERRY That's because you can't appreciate early drama. Stage drama. Of course the masks were symbolic, that's difficult to understand.

MASON I would have liked to have been there with Orestes. Katherine ... we shall go there, someday. See the Parthenon. Hear the classic plays in Greek.

MRS. TURNER-MASON: Yes Henry. That would be nice. Very nice, Henry, if you say so.

TERRY I liked the bull-fighting in Spain. Even Toledo. I liked walking through those narrow, cobbled streets ... listening to the language spoken, soft and lilting ... seeing patches of lawn in patios where you least expect it. It was like a world apart. Apart from modern technology.

MATILDA That's where that greasy, dirty old man tried to pick you up? Hah!

TERRY What do you mean, greasy, dirty old man? He wasn't that old!

CHAD He'll never see forty again!

TERRY (Mad.) That's a lie! A lie! You're jealous. Plain jealous ...

CHAD (Shouts.) Jealous! Why? Of that old man? He had shifty eyes! He wasn't the criminal type I'm used to drawing. Oh no! A criminal has loneliness ... fear or sadness in his eyes. But that old goon, his eyes shifted. It was cold ... cowardly shifty eyes. Didn't you see his shifty eyes, or behind it ... shift-shift.

TERRY (Shrieking with rage.) Oh ... Oh ... damn you, Chadwick Turner! Male chauvinist!

MRS. TURNER-MASON: (Horrified.) Oh ... Chad, Terry! Let's ... let's calm down.

CHAD Sorry mother, dad. I guess we've had a slew of quarrels. (Laughs; both laugh.) Sorry Terry. I don't know what came over me, what comes over me, what happens when ... can't figure it out. Sorry. (He kisses her cheek, smooths her hair.)

MATILDA Did you go over to Africa?

MASON Africa?

TERRY No, Matilda. We did not go to Africa. We flew to Greece, non-stop from San Francisco, Washington, D.C., Rome, Greece. Well ... a ten hour stop-over in Rome.

CHAD   I liked Florence.

MATILDA Florence? Who's she? Ennybody I know? (Everybody grins.)

CHAD   (Affectionately.) Florence is a city in Italy.

MATILDA My, my. Florence. Was it pretty?

CHAD   I liked it better than Rome. It was a small city, intimate ... Less a tourist town. And there were life-size statues on pedestals, some with, and some without fig leaves.

MATILDA You don't say. My, my. Must have been a pretty sight.

TERRY   (Sarcastically.) It looked a bit naked.

CHAD   (Irritably.) What's wrong with that?

TERRY   Nothing. Nothing. Who said anything about right or wrong? You've become so jumpy. I just made a comment ... a personal opinion. I didn't know that would start an argument. (Pushes her chair and gets up, crosses to bay window, *stage-left* and peers out window.)

MASON Well, I must be leaving for my class. We're reading "The Patriots" in front of a television camera. (Chuckles.) At last. I've stumbled on the solution. Students will read anything for television. Even the worst students. I got to 'em! I did! They'll read thousands of words, if they know they can rewrite a small part for themselves to act in front of a TV camera.

MATILDA Atta boy, professor. Personally, a swift kick would be better, but den, dat's jest my personal opinion. (All laugh.)

MASON The play has long, dramatic lines. I do my share by looking the part of Thomas Jefferson. That way, I know, they know, that we'll get a TV camera. Oh, Katherine, Mrs. Jefferson is ... well, you don't need to come today, but ... tomorrow, another dry run.

MRS. TURNER-MASON I wish I could read a book and write a dancing role for myself.

MASON You are splendid just as you are, Katherine. No dancing.

MATILDA Hey, if I could read ... one thousand words ... wow, dat's a whole lot of comic books. (All laugh.)

CHAD (Laughing.) I haven't laughed like this for a long time.

MASON Well, I must be going. Terry! (Terry goes to him like a lost child. He hugs and comforts her.) There, Mrs. Turner! Promise me you won't bite my son's head off. (Terry has fingered his costume, then starts to bawl.) What's the matter, Terry? (She breaks away, runs to *stairway, upstage-center,* exits.) She loves you Chad.

CHAD I know, dad. Love is ... I love her, too. (He exits *stairway* after her.)

MASON (Bussing his wife.) Bye dear. Now don't start bawling. I'll bring home *Wonder Woman* to make you laugh. (Exits *downstage-left.*) Bye Matilda. (Matilda responds gaily as she goes about busily.)

MRS. TURNER-MASON (At the baywindow.) Look at him walk like Thomas Jefferson. Sometimes, Matilda ... sometimes, I wonder how two people ... well my first husband was different from me, yet, at the same time, we did have some common interests ... and on the other hand. (Sighs.) Sometimes marriage seems a bit complicated, don't you think so, Matilda?

MATILDA Sometimes? (Chuckles.) Seems lak it's one continual battle.

MRS. TURNER-MASON (Laughs.) You are very funny to have around. I often wondered what would I do ... without you. You're part of my life. (Wanders to bookcase.)

MATILDA Oh, you'll survive. You always will, Mrs. Turner. I guess, we, both of us. We get knocked down, but somehow we jumps back.

MRS. TURNER-MASON Is that what life is about, a yo-yo?

MATILDA Yep. Up and down. And sometimes, one has to do practical things, think practical. When you think practical, you do practical.

MRS. TURNER-MASON (Thinks for a moment philosophically, and takes a book from the bookshelf.) Hm-m-m. Looks like heavy reading. If I don't like this *Hairy Ape,* I'm going to tell him so. (Matilda laughs. Mrs. Turner walks slowly to the rocker *downstage-left.* Lights dim. Matilda starts singing and ad-libs to herself. Blackout.)

ACT II
Scene 3

The Scene:

The Masons', that evening.

Stage Directions:

Matilda is working in the kitchenette humming "Nobody knows de trouble I've seen," with body language—head shaking/heaving sighs—added to her ad-libs to herself. Arguing is heard *off-stage* by Lorna and Sam, "You did, yes you did; no I didn't; yes you did, did, did; No, no." Matilda picks up the song idea—Yes, my baby, no sir, no my baby, yes, sir ... dances the Charleston to boot. Enter Lorna and Sam, back door *stage-right.*

MATILDA Hiya luvbirds! Well ... (Lorna has dropped her hat box and Sam his suitcase. Sam takes Lorna aside.) Whose luggage may dis be, pray tell? I'd like to be informed, as soon as you get through chit-chatting.

SAM Lorna. Wat's de use. I don't like Jason, but I'll try.

LORNA You did! Did, did, did! Oh ... How could you?

SAM I got mad. He don't help do dishes, neither, but dat's nuthin'. I promise. I'll ... I'll ... I'll ...

LORNA You didn't have to ... insult him. He's my brudder.

SAM I know, you're not like him.

LORNA He's my brudder.

SAM If I had called him a zebra, mebbe.

LORNA There you go again, thinking up names. (She snorts and stomps out, exits *stage-right.*)

MATILDA And whose luggage may dis be?

SAM Miss Terry.

MATILDA Wrong house, she don't live here no more.

SAM De way she and Chad were billin' 'n' cooin', she's coming right over.

MATILDA Wow! They got troubles?

SAM Not like mine. Not like mine. Terry don't like Chad's beard.

MATILDA Don't blem Terry. Don't mind bear-hugs myself, but bear kisses, dat's sum'in' else. (Thinks.) Wat's yore trouble Sam? Tell mama.

SAM Jason, Lorna's brudder.

MATILDA Oh, in-laws, I know. Couldn't stand my in-laws neither. But you have only one. I had four generations ... mudder-in-law telling me how to cook ... grandmudder telling me how to clean de house ... and great-grandmudder yelling, she was plumb crazy livin' wid my in-laws so long.

SAM (Laughs.) Lorna's brudder ... Jason. (Seriously.) Jason went to college.

MATILDA College, oh.

SAM The Sanford School of Business.

MATILDA Wow! You don't say! SANFORD. Real Classy. Lotta Nobel prizefighters dere.

SAM Lorna worked all dese years.

MATILDA Oh? Baby brudder Jason?

SAM He keeps borrowin' money yet.

MATILDA No kidding. Time for him to get a job. Get off his hindsite.

SAM He ain't got the right job, he sez. And he ain't got no job ... yet ... he kips tellin' me how to earn a living. Dat fathead, jackass!

MATILDA In-laws. I know, Sam. So I left mine behind, high-tailed it outtar dem hills of Kentucky. Never looked back. If I didn't have lady luck smile on me and de Turners, I'd jump ovah de Golden Gate. But ... Here I am. Here I stay. Lorna loves you, Sam. And you love her. So wat, if you have to listen to ejucated in-laws on welfare. Close yore ears! (*Off-stage* Lorna is yelling SAMMMUEL ... Samuel Bull Grant. I'm waiting!) Hear dat? I toldya she loves you. Hurry!

SAM (Yells.) Coming, Lorna. (Affectionately.) You're a pal, Matilda, thanks. (Exits back door, *stage-right.* Enter Terry front door, *stage-left.*)

TERRY Where's dad, Matilda?

MATILDA Good evening, Miss Terry. Dey went to see a musical ... "Destry Rides Again." Mrs. Turner-Mason likes cowboys.

TERRY I'm staying here tonight.

MATILDA Yes ma'm. I'll turn down the covers in your old room. (She starts to exit *upstage stairway.*)

TERRY (Shrieks.) MATILLLDA! (Matilda jumps suddenly, turns speechless.) Tell me something!

MATILDA I better sit in de rockin' chair. My legs don't feel so good. (Goes to rocking chair near the bay window, *stage-left.*)

TERRY (Explodes.) DAMMMMM-NATION!

MATILDA (Compassionately.) Terry! (Terry runs to her and bawls on her knees.) Dere, dere child! Seems lak you is havin' troubles lak all young brides. (Terry bawls louder.) Mebbe you ken think of somethin' pleasant ... lak yore trip to Europe. (Terry moans a bit.) Florence ... and dem figleaf statues, and dem widout fig leaves. (Terry laughs and then continues sniffling.) ... and dem Greek plays which mak no sense except Orestes. (Terry moans a little more) and dem narrow crook'd hobblestones in Spain. (Terry howls.) Wat's de matter child? Didn't you enjoy yore honeymoon?

TERRY (Laughs, cries, shakes her head, finally blows her nose and regains her composure.) We bicycled everywhere, so Chad could draw things, people ... not the best looking ... not the cleanest ... nor healthiest.

MATILDA Third class ... people?

TERRY Just about, we bicycled everywhere.

MATILDA Well ... ain't bicycling fun?

TERRY On your honeymoon?

MATILDA You did stop to eat 'n' ... to sleep?

TERRY How could we?

MATILDA (Diplomatically.) I'd get mighty weak if I don't eat.

TERRY (Remembering.) Oh ... yes, we did have fun at first, flying to Greece ... staying at a fine hotel, dressing up and eating out in elegant restaurants, sometimes out of the way tiny cubby-hole of a restaurant, but the food was excellent, wines superb. We slept in a real bedroom ... made you feel you were on a honeymoon. Going to see the plays in the amphitheatre, yes ... that was fun. (Remembers unpleasant memories.) But when we flew to Madrid, we started bicycling. Up and down mountains. (Irritated.) I was sick and tired of hostels ... and saddle sores. (Begins to sniffle again.) Matilda ...

MATILDA Yes, Terry.

TERRY I'm mad at Chad.

MATILDA I can see dat. Was you mad wid Chad wen you was on de bicycle?

MATILDA (Nods.) Yes.

MATILDA Den wat did you do?

TERRY I'd bicycle as fast as I could ... in the wrong direction.

MATILDA (Relieved.) Mus' have been a tiring honeymoon. But you all jest flew in dis mornin'. Mebbe after a rest, you won't be mad?

TERRY I don't like fighting. I can't seem to say the right words, diplomatically.

MATILDA It takes time to understand people, but if you love someone, you can work out problems. (Doorbell chimes. Terry rises and runs quickly, stairways *center-stage,* exits. Matilda opens the front door, *stage-left.* Enter Chad. He has shaven his beard and looks youthful and forlorn.)

CHAD Is Terry here, Matilda?

MATILDA Oh ... my, you looks ... oh, yes, yes, she's here. Said she loves you, yet fightin' words come between you.

CHAD She said that?

MATILDA And a bit more.

CHAD Did she tell you ... everything?

MATILDA No, jest the part, you and she ... nice cubbyhole restaurants in Greece, and sitting on the rocks in the amphitheatre ... and 'bout bicycling in Spain, ups and downs ... real tiring.

CHAD (Bitterly.) Funny, I thought I understood people. Weak people, strong people, poor people, rich people ... even sad people.

MATILDA Hard to understan' mad people like Terry?

CHAD Impossible! (He paces back and forth.)

MATILDA Rockin' chair, here I come. (Goes to rocking chair and sits.)

CHAD She's spoiled — absolutely spoiled.

MATILDA She's nineteen.

CHAD So ...

MATILDA She's young. She's still in her teens, practically.

CHAD Always wanting to dress up ... to go places ... to be seen, not to see, or enjoy what there is to see.

MATILDA She'll grow.

CHAD Never. She was born spoiled.

MATILDA She loves you, Chad. Mebbe, lak Professor Mason sez, she has too much imagination.

CHAD (Ironically.) What good is imagination? You have to deal with the real world ... real people ... real facts.

MATILDA (Sighing.) If I was somebody, not nobody ... mebbe I'd know answers, ken work out problems, lak Professor Mason. He has terrific logic. All I have ... is hoss sense.

CHAD (Grinning.) Matilda ... you and mother are real artists, more so than I. I just draw people. I can't communicate with them. I don't understand them any more. I don't know what's to happen, where I'm going ...

MATILDA If I could draw a picture ... I'd say you goin' upstairs to rest.

CHAD (Remembering.) Oh! Oh! (He goes quickly to *stairway center-stage* and stops abruptly, turns slowly.) Matilda?

MATILDA What?

CHAD You're a treasure.

MATILDA Yeh! King Solomon's gold mine. (Both laugh. Chad exits upstairs. Matilda exuberantly crosses *downstage-right* to the dining table to write a message.) Gotta leave a message for de old folks. (Thinks, then laughs to herself as she writes.) Yeh! Why not? I ain't much of a poet, but my teachers used to say: "Matilda, you got lip talent. If you can write down what yore lip says, you'll be famous lak dat eccentric Emily Dickinson." Now, if I ken remember how to spell. (Laughs to herself as she writes. Lights dim, then blackout.)

The Scene:

The Masons', still later that evening.

Stage Directions:

Offstage voices of Mrs. Turner-Mason and Professor Mason are heard arguing. That wasn't the best. It was,
I thought. No, it wasn't. If you say so, Henry. Enter front
door, *stage-left*. Both are dressed in evening attire, 1980.
They look elegant.

MASON The next time we go to the theatre ... I'd like to
hear the actors with decent dialogue, oh, I don't
care if they speak like country bumpkins but
with choice words, meaningful. Maybe a tinkling
piano, or soft violins in the background, but no
brass. "Destry Rides Again" was brassy. Deaf-
ening. (Shakes head.) I have a headache now.

MRS. TURNER-MASON Oh dear, I'm sorry Henry. For
your headache. (Brightly.) But didn't you enjoy
the dance scenes? All those modern dancers
on ... on one leg hopping about, as if they were
on horses?

MASON I'm not complaining. I enjoyed the musical. I like music. But the brass in the orchestra. It was too loud. I couldn't think. If they had used the brass for clippity clops, soft hoofs, hoofs running in the distance ... Oh, my head.

MRS. TURNER-MASON Look at this luggage.

MASON What?

MRS. TURNER-MASON Luggage. And here's a note. From Matilda. (Reads and laughs.)

MASON What's so funny?

MRS. TURNER-MASON The note is from Matilda. Matilda doesn't spell very well, but she's a real poet when it comes to imagery. Surrealistic imagery? Mimicry?

MASON Whatever is that?

MRS. TURNER-MASON It's modern poetry, that's what it is. Direct to the point. Here Henry. (Gives him the note.)

MASON (Imitation of Matilda.) Woods ya know, dat after da storm, lak homin' pijuns ... wouldn't ya know dat instinct brung dem to roost. Plop, plop. Not lak ordinary birds, but specialized breeds, dem birds of de boomarang fedder, lak loss yung ones, dey cum home. Love is ... to ride de storms. Sh-h-h-h! Dey's restin'. No harm done. Let dem rest. Ho hum ... Matilda.

MRS. TURNER-MASON What do you think?

MASON Damn those brass. I still can't think. (Looks at note.) Modern poetry is not my forte. I could never understand the poet, T.S. Eliot. Worse still, his interpreters. This reads like ad-libs to Matilda's songs. I'm trying to hear the song that goes with it. (Starts to hum "Short'nin' Bread" to fit the note.)

MRS. TURNER-MASON (Laughing gaily.) Oh Henry. That's impossible.

MASON (Laughs.) Well it doesn't fit Honey-suckle Rose.

MRS. TURNER-MASON My dear Henry. I love you, but you are so logical. It is just a tender feeling poets try to create, and sometimes they can't say it ... perfectly, but if the message comes across, and the tenderness is felt ... then you have a poem. Isn't it amazing?

MASON Katherine, in a few words ... can you interpret this feeling Matilda is trying to create? I don't understand Matilda's poetry.

MRS. TURNER-MASON Yes Henry. (Reads and nods and smiles mischievously.) It says ... poetically, that Terry and Chad are upstairs, so ... sh-h-h ... don't argue too loudly tonight. (Innocently.) Isn't that sweet?

MASON (Sighing.) Thank you Katherine. Modern poetry ... is enigmatic. (Chuckles.) I'll have to take your word for it. Why do you suppose ...

MRS. TURNER-MASON (Giggles.) Sh-h-h-h. (She takes his hand, they stumble and giggle, exit stairway *upstage center* sh-h-hing each other.)

CURTAINS

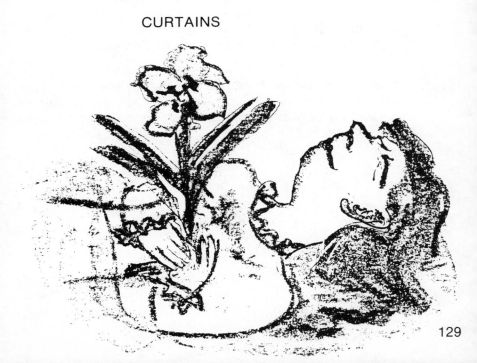

APPENDIX

Susan Thorley Schwafel holds Bachelor of Arts and Master of Arts degrees in English. She is the author of *Modern Theatre Interpreted in Terms of Dr. Carl Jung's Theory of the Archetypes of Character,* published in 1974. This book can be ordered by writing her at 730 Anderson Drive, Los Altos, Ca. 94022. She has taught literature for several years on a college level and holds a California Community College Instructor's Credential in the language arts and literature.

May Kapela Davenport studied Drawing and Painting at Columbia University and at the Corcoran Gallery of Art. Her paintings were exhibited as cultural presentations of an American Artist at the United States Information Center in Calcutta, India in July 1959 and in Georgetown, Guyana in February 1968. She received her Bachelor of Arts degree in Drawing and Painting from George Washington University, and earned her teaching credentials in elementary and secondary education at San Jose State University, San Jose, California. She enjoys writing as well as drawing and painting.

Sketches on pages 1, 38, 70 and 129 by May Davenport were from a collection of slide illustrations created to accompany taped lectures in General Psychology by Lorraine Dieudonne, Foothill College, Los Altos Hills, California.